THE SHORTEST JOURNEY

THE SHORTEST JOURNEY

Hazel Holt

Chivers Press • G.K. Hall & Co.
Bath, Avon, England   Thorndike, Maine USA

This Large Print edition is published by Chivers Press, England, and by G.K. Hall & Co., USA.

Published in 1995 in the U.K. by arrangement with Macmillan Publishers Limited.

Published in 1995 in the U.S. by arrangement with St. Martin's Press, Inc.

U.K. Hardcover   ISBN 0–7451–2984–6 (Chivers Large Print)
U.K. Softcover   ISBN 0–7451–2995–1 (Camden Large Print)
U.S. Softcover   ISBN 0–7838–1138–1 (Nightingale Collection Edition)

The text of this Large Print edition is unabridged.
Other aspects of the book may vary from the original edition.

Set in 16 pt. New Times Roman.

Printed in Great Britain on acid-free paper.

British Library Cataloguing in Publication Data available

Library of Congress Cataloging-in-Publication Data

Holt, Hazel, 1928–
  The shortest journey / Hazel Holt.
    p.   cm.
  ISBN 0–7838–1138–1 (lg. print : sc)
  1. Large type books.   I. Title.
[PR6058.O473S56   1995]
823'.914—dc20   94–37507

For Joy

THE SHORTEST JOURNEY

CHAPTER ONE

'Is a good family,' Mrs Jankiewicz said, 'but there is no title.'

She was silent for a moment, contemplating this insurmountable flaw and I said quickly, 'But Sophie is very happy with him.'

'Oh, *happy*.' Mrs Jankiewicz shrugged.

'And,' I pursued, 'he *is* Polish and a Roman Catholic.'

'Is true,' she admitted. 'Zofia'—she gave her daughter's name its proper pronunciation—'is a good Polish girl. She would not marry a foreigner.'

We both sat quietly drinking our tea. It was a conversation we had had many times. Zofia Jankiewicz (now Zofia Borowska) was no longer a girl—she was my contemporary and I was now in my middle fifties—and she had been married for twenty years. But to the elderly no topic of conversation is ever quite finished; it can be brought out again and again, and each time a little more can be added to it.

'His father was a captain with General Zajac in Tehran. His uncle was an attaché in London. Was a good family.'

She was silent again and I looked round the room with my customary feeling of sadness. It was quite a good-sized room and had a nice view of the sea (that was one of the pleasant features of West Lodge, which made it superior to the other nursing homes in Taviscombe) but it was woefully inadequate to house all the objects that Mrs Jankiewicz had brought with her from her large house in Park Walk. Mrs Wilmot, the Matron, had tried to protest as, under Mrs Jankiewicz's brisk supervision, ornamental rugs were nailed up on the walls, large pieces of ornately carved furniture were heaved into place and a multiplicity of heavy silver objects was distributed about the room. But such was the force of the old lady's personality (although half-blind with cataracts and practically crippled with arthritis) that she was allowed to create around her in this unpromising setting a sort of little Poland-in-miniature. True, the staff muttered a little as they moved the objects to dust—but they did so under their breath, since Mrs Jankiewicz held autocratic views on domestic staff and they were all decidedly in awe of her.

'Do you want some more tea, Sheila?' she asked. 'I will ring for the girl. Alas, I cannot give you proper tea in this place.'

We both turned our heads and looked at the silver samovar sitting on a small table. That had been one battle she had not won. I regarded the samovar with affection. When I was a girl and had gone to tea with Sophie—we had been at school together—it had always seemed to me the most glamorous object imaginable. Indeed, the whole household was so different and so much more exciting than any other I had ever known. Dr Jankiewicz was a delightful man, quiet and agreeable, amused, I thought, by his exuberant wife, whose exotic conversation and foreign ways fascinated me. Sophie was simply my friend. English at school and 'a good Polish girl' at home, she led two lives, as all second-generation refugees seemed to do.

But now Dr Jankiewicz was dead, and Sophie, who had also become a doctor, was married and living in Canada with her husband. Sophie had wanted her mother to go to Canada with them, but Mrs Jankiewicz had been firm.

'Not another country,' she said. 'First was Poland, then Siberia, then Persia, then Lebanon, then England. I stay in England.'

With her usual resolute practicality she had sold her house, forced a large number of objects upon a reluctant Sophie ('Honestly, Sheila, it's going to cost more to ship them out to Nova Scotia than all our fares put together! And where on earth are we going to put them in our apartment?') and settled herself in at West Lodge. Here she rapidly gained ascendancy, so that after only a few months she was recognised as Chief Resident and both the other residents and the staff were, on the whole, proud of her, rather as one might be of a cumbersome but rare and valuable piece of furniture whose prestige compensates for its awkwardness.

I was very fond of her, not only because I had reached the age when I valued things and people connected with my youth, but also for her own unique blend of warmth and eccentricity.

'Mr Williams's son came yesterday,' she said. 'Is a bad man, not good to his father. He comes only when he wants something—money, of course, for that business of his. But is throwing the good money after the bad—he will never make it pay because he does not work hard. Is wrong to give him more and I tell Mr Williams this, but he not listen to anyone, even to me.'

Mrs Jankiewicz had channelled her still considerable energy into evolving an information system that made M15 look like pitiful amateurs. She called it taking an interest. But hers was a benevolent autocracy; she was always on the look-out for wrongs done to any of the other old people.

'Someone must see to their rights,' she would say. 'Is only me; their children do not care. They were not brought up well, like my Zofia.'

'Yes,' I said. 'I saw Mr Williams's son the last time he came to see the old man. He struck me as a nasty piece of work, smarming round Matron and saying how lovely everything was.'

Mrs Jankiewicz snorted. 'He cannot have

4

seen the dust in his father's room. I went in there last week to tell him to come down to dinner with me and it was terrible. Was *thick*, everywhere. Is that girl Glenda, lazy, only thinking about boys! I have to tell her many times about the dust.'

For someone with a sight problem Mrs Jankiewicz had an apparently miraculous ability to spot dust, grimy paintwork or the wrong shade of blue in a bed-jacket purchased at her command by one of the staff.

I sought to change the subject to one less controversial. 'What lovely flowers! Those chrysanthemums are such a beautiful shade of dusky pink.'

Her face softened. 'Are pretty—from Mrs Rossiter. She went shopping yesterday and bought them for me for a present to cheer me up, she said, because today is ten years since my poor Stanislas is dead. Mrs Rossiter is a kind person. You are kind, too,' she said, taking my hand in hers. 'You come to see me because you remember.'

'He was such a dear man,' I said. 'I was so fond of him. And I know that one never stops missing them.'

I too am a widow. My husband, Peter, died three years ago.

'I do not think Mrs Rossiter misses her husband,' Mrs Jankiewicz said. 'That man was not a nice person at all.'

I thought of Colonel Rossiter, a cold,

unfriendly, ill-tempered man, and said, 'No, he was horrid; she was well rid of him. I did think that after he died she might have managed to have a more enjoyable life, but then she developed this heart trouble…'

Mrs Jankiewicz snorted again. 'Is not *trouble*,' she said. 'She is quite able to do things but they do not let her. If I have no more than that wrong with me then I would not be in this place but in my own home.'

'But Thelma was very concerned about her mother—living in London and with a career, she couldn't get down very often. She thought her mother would be safer here, where people can keep an eye on her.'

'Too many people keep an eye in this place,' Mrs Jankiewicz said. 'Is no privacy.'

I reflected that Mrs Jankiewicz's own eyes (albeit dimmed with cataracts) contributed considerably to the residents' lack of privacy.

'Never,' she continued, 'does she have any choice, poor Mrs Rossiter, never any *freedom*.' Her voice rose on this evocative word. 'Always she must be doing what other people tell her, first her husband—that nasty man—now her children. Is no life, and now she is old and has never known freedom. I would not have been so. In Siberia I was more free than she is.'

I was used to Mrs Jankiewicz's tendency to dramatise things but I felt this was going a bit far.

'Oh, I don't think it's *that* bad. I'm sure she

6

doesn't mind being here too much. I mean, she's quite active and can get about. She gets a taxi to go shopping in Taunton. She even went up to London to a matinée last year. Thelma met her at Paddington—they went to Covent Garden. She had a lovely day.'

'She did not want to go to Covent Garden,' Mrs Jankiewicz said. 'She does not like the ballet. She want to see a show by that man Noël someone...'

'Noël Coward?'

'Is in some small place, not grand like Covent Garden. Thelma not like places that are not grand.'

'Still, it was a day out for her.'

'But not what she *want*!' Mrs Jankiewicz rounded off her circular argument, as she so often did, triumphantly.

'Well, anyway...' I gathered my gloves and bag and prepared to depart. 'I thought I'd just pop in and see her now, while I'm here.'

'Is good. She will enjoy to see you,' she said benevolently.

We embraced each other warmly and I went out into the corridor and up the stairs to Mrs Rossiter's room. I knocked and a low voice murmured something which I took to be an invitation to go in.

The room that I now entered was in complete contrast to the one I had just left. Where Mrs Jankiewicz had surrounded herself with reminders of her past, Mrs Rossiter's

7

room seemed almost bare. True, it was comfortably furnished, as all the rooms in that very expensive nursing home were, but the general effect was impersonal, like a well-designed hotel room. The only pieces of furniture that she had brought with her from her old home were a small desk of Regency design made of some dark wood with little gilded sphinxes for feet, a footstool covered in petit-point, a rather beautiful eighteenth-century French clock, a watercolour of Table Mountain in a simple gilt frame and a small ivory figure of a gazelle. The only other personal touches in the room were several pots of flowering plants and two photographs. One—the larger of the two—was a studio portrait of her daughter Thelma, a strikingly handsome woman with dark hair and large dark eyes. The other was a framed snapshot of a nondescript-looking man, youngish, fairish, unremarkable. This was her son Alan. She was sitting in a chair by the window but got to her feet to greet me as I came into the room.

'Sheila!' she cried. 'What a lovely surprise!'

As I gave her a hug I was dismayed to feel how much more frail she seemed since the last time I had seen her.

'How are you?' I asked with real concern.

'Oh, I'm splendid,' she said, 'absolutely splendid.'

'You look rather pale.'

'I've had a bit of a cold and that's kept me

8

indoors. Now that I can get out and about again I'll soon perk up. Just a little walk along the beach and I'll be right as rain.'

'It doesn't look too inviting at the moment,' I said, looking out of the window at the long stretch of sand, deserted and raked by wind and driving rain, and at the iron grey waves breaking in white lines on the shingle further along. 'You're better off indoors today.'

'Yes, indeed. I'm very lucky to be here all safe and snug and warm, when you think of how some poor souls of my age have to live...'

Her voice, which was always soft and hesitant, died away.

'You're settled in all right, I see.'

'Oh, yes. Everyone has been so good— Thelma arranged everything. So difficult for her, having to come down from London every time. And Gordon has been wonderful. He came when Thelma couldn't get away— though of course they couldn't both be away from the office at the same time.'

'Ah, yes, of course,' I said.

Thelma and her husband Gordon owned a high-powered, very successful advertising agency and had the sort of lifestyle that I only knew about from television commercials.

'I see you've brought some of your things with you,' I said. 'It's nice to have something familiar around you—it makes it seem more home-like.'

'Yes, just a few odds and ends. As Thelma

9

said, I don't want to clutter up the room with too much stuff.'

'Yes, it's not very big, really, after all those enormous rooms at the Manor.'

'Oh, I'm very comfortable,' she said hastily. 'And it's got a lovely view—I do so love the sea.'

'I'm glad you brought that little Regency desk,' I said. 'It's so pretty—I've always admired it, ever since I was a child. I remember, when Mother and I used to come to tea—when I was very young—I used to sit on the floor and stroke the sphinxes!'

She smiled. 'Your mother was so kind to me, I used to love your visits. You were such a solemn little thing, very quiet and shy—not like Thelma.'

I remembered Thelma as a child. She always took the lead in any activity, as if by right; I always felt that her peremptory manner was displeasing and unsuitable in one who was several years my junior. Alan was younger still, despised accordingly by his older sister, and never allowed to participate in any of our games.

Mrs Rossiter laid a loving hand on the desk. 'It *is* charming, isn't it? Fancy you loving it all those years ago. I shall leave it to you in my will.'

'Oh, no, you mustn't,' I said, deeply embarrassed. 'I mean, I couldn't possibly...'

'Nonsense, my dear, I would like to think of

10

it having a loving home when I am gone.'

'No, really, you can't—Thelma...'

'Thelma took all the pieces she wanted when the Manor was sold.'

'Well, Alan might...'

'Alan's abroad so much and when he is here he's got no proper home to put anything in, just that tiny flat in Earl's Court.'

I never quite knew what Alan did—something to do with helping the Third World, digging wells or advising on crops. It all sounded very worthy but I got the impression that he hadn't been inspired by any burning desire to help the underprivileged, but had simply drifted into it when he couldn't think of anything else to do.

'No, Sheila dear, there's no one else I would rather have it. Accept it for your dear mother's sake, if for nothing else!'

My mother always had a soft spot for Mrs Rossiter. 'That poor little soul!' she called her. So we would quite often go to tea at the Manor—a gloomy seventeenth-century house with dark panelling and heavily leaded windows through which the light filtered greenly. I was a nervous child and Thelma used to delight in reminding me that the house was said to be haunted. I can still feel the slippery polished wood of the great staircase under my feet as I scuttled down the stairs from the gloom of the nursery passage to the blessed lights of the ground floor below and the reassuring presence of the grown-ups.

'Well,' I said hesitantly, 'it's very sweet of you ... but you mustn't start talking about wills, you know.'

'At my age, my dear, it is quite natural. I'll drop a line to Mr Robertson.'

To change the subject I said, 'I've just been to see Mrs Jankiewicz. She was in splendid form!'

Mrs Rossiter laughed. 'She certainly keeps everyone here on their toes—I do envy her positive attitude to everything!'

'I suppose, after all she's been through, she simply takes each day as it comes and gets what she can out of it. And she certainly seems to enjoy life, even now.'

'It is a great gift—almost the greatest. I had thought that now I'm old life would be simple, there would be no problems—but, somehow there are...'

She sat by the window looking at but not seeing two figures in raincoats battling along the promenade against the wind, while a small dog ran round them in circles.

She suddenly recollected herself and asked, 'How is Michael?'

'He's in London now, at the College of Law. I was delighted, as you can imagine, when he said he wanted to be a solicitor. Peter would have been so pleased.'

'He's a dear boy—you're very lucky.'

'I know. I honestly don't know how I would

have got through when Mother died, and then Peter, so soon after, if it hadn't been for Michael. When you have children you know you've got to carry on, for their sake.'

She gave me a warm smile but didn't say anything and I recollected that that had hardly been the situation when her husband died. It was Thelma, then, who had taken charge. As she had done ever since.

We chatted a little about the old days and I was just on the point of leaving when there was a tap at the door and, not waiting for a reply, a small, sturdy figure came into the room.

Annie Fisher was what used to be known as a 'treasure'. She had been employed at the Manor for all of Mrs Rossiter's married life. Beginning as a kitchen maid before the war, she had ended up running the whole establishment practically single-handed, since the Manor was really quite isolated and it was impossible to get any sort of living-in help. She had even nursed Colonel Rossiter during his last illness and that couldn't have been easy, because he was difficult and tiresome enough when in full health and I couldn't imagine that he was a particularly good patient. After he died, it was her energy and devotion that had made it possible for Mrs Rossiter to go on living at the Manor as long as she had done. A really admirable person, then, who had given her life selflessly to the care of her employers— and yet I always had a slight feeling of distaste

13

whenever I met her. I can't explain it—a sort of Dr Fell thing, Peter used to say, when I told him, and really it was as irrational as that.

She crossed the room, moved a chair near to Mrs Rossiter and sat down beside her. 'Well, m'dear, and how are you today? Got company, I see. That's nice.' She turned her rather prominent pale blue eyes towards me. 'Isn't it good of Mrs Malory to come and see you?'

I began to feel my customary irritation.

Annie Fisher started rummaging in her large shopping-bag. 'There, m'dear, I brought some of those biscuits you like and a refill for your pen, like you asked me to get. And shall I take those nightdresses back and wash them? I don't think they do them properly here. I mean, they do their best but that very fine cotton does need proper ironing...'

I got to my feet. 'Well,' I said, 'I'll leave you in Annie's capable hands.'

'It was lovely to see you, Sheila dear. Come again when you can...'

Because Annie's chair was pushed right up against Mrs Rossiter's, I couldn't get near to give her my usual farewell hug so I simply waved goodbye from the doorway. Before I had shut the door behind me I could hear Annie once again in full flow.

I walked along the impersonal corridor towards the front door, feeling rather crossly that I had been edged out. But as I stepped out of the hothouse temperature of West Lodge

14

and into the brisk, not to say chilly, breeze blowing in from the sea-front, I pulled myself together and reminded myself that poor Annie had nothing else in her life; it was very mean-minded of me to begrudge her Mrs Rossiter's time and attention. After all, when the Manor was sold she had gone to live in a small council flat in Taviscombe, and how she employed her still considerable energies I didn't really know. I knew that Mrs Rossiter would have made sure she had a good pension, but she had no family near—just a brother in Australia whom she used to talk about with pride, since he had 'got on'. But time must hang heavily on her hands, and what could be more natural than that she should pop in quite often to see her old employer? Not that one could really think of Mrs Rossiter as anything as positive as an employer and I am sure that after Colonel Rossiter died (he had been decidedly imperious and treated all servants as potentially mutinous troops who had to be kept under strict control) Annie had run things more or less her own way. Thelma, at that time, was only too thankful to have a reliable person to look after her mother. Anyway, Annie always made a great fuss of Thelma and, in the old days, had waged fearful feuds with Thelma's Nanny Philips.

I walked through the Jubilee Gardens, noting that a lot of the beds were bare now and freshly dug for the winter; just a few contained some sad late chrysanthemums that the early frosts hadn't bitten off. My mood of irritation was now replaced by one of melancholy.

It seemed today that everything was drawing to a close, not just the year. Mrs Jankiewicz and Mrs Rossiter were almost the last of Mother's friends—so many others had died—and when they were gone yet more links with my past would be broken; one day soon there would be no one who still thought of me as a child. Then I would be forced to feel really grown up at last. I felt somehow diminished and sad.

An elderly man, walking rather unsteadily and being enthusiastically pulled along by a small grey poodle on a lead, greeted me as I approached.

'Hello, Mrs Malory—splendid day, isn't it? Nice and fresh, blows the cobwebs away. It's grand to be out!'

Mr Sewell was a retired accountant, a widower, who had been one of the most active of our Red Cross helpers until he had a stroke six months ago.

'*Well*!' I said. 'You're looking marvellous! How nice to see you out and about again!'

'Oh yes, nothing wrong with me. I'll soon be back in harness again—you tell them! Got to get on—Bijou likes her walk, doesn't like to be kept standing about.'

Bijou gave a little plunge forward, like an eager horse at the starting gate, and they were away.

I turned my head to see them go and smiled. My animals would be waiting, eager to hear the sound of my key in the lock, the dogs rushing into the hall barking ecstatically, Foss, my Siamese, picking his way delicately downstairs as if to disassociate himself from the over-exuberance of their welcome. I walked briskly towards the market to buy Foss's coley and perhaps some potted shrimps as a treat for me. Soon it would be December and Michael would be home for the holidays. My mood lightened at the prospect.

CHAPTER TWO

I didn't see Mrs Rossiter for several months after that. I was away for a bit and then there was Christmas and then I had flu and then *she* had flu—quite badly—and, before I knew where the winter had gone, it was spring and the primroses were out all round the banks of the orchard. I thought that I really must take some in for her—she always said that they were her favourite flower. These thoughts were going through my mind in Smiths as I stood looking at the primroses and violets, which together with lambs and stylised silver crosses decorated the Easter cards.

'Aren't they pretty!' a soft voice said and

there was Mrs Rossiter standing behind me. She was wearing a tweed winter coat and, although it wasn't a very thick one, it seemed to hang heavily from her shoulders. She had lost weight and her thin neck looked painfully fragile inside the deep collar.

'How lovely to see you!' I exclaimed. 'And how marvellous that you are out and about again.'

'Well, it's my first little visit to the shops but I wanted to get a birthday card for Thelma—she's fifty-one on Wednesday. Can you believe it!'

'Only too well, since I'm four years older! Look, have you got half an hour? Shall we go and have some coffee?'

Her face lit up. 'Oh, that *would* be nice. You can help me choose a card; I'm never really sure what Thelma likes these days! I never seemed to get her presents right, even when she was a little girl—so now I just send her a cheque to get herself a little something.'

'Well, it is rather fun to have some extra money just to splurge with,' I said, though I knew very well that Thelma was not the splurging kind.

We pondered long over the choice of a card—Mrs Rossiter leaning towards idyllic country landscapes ('To remind her of the country now she's shut up in London') while I felt that Thelma would like those rather smart 'thirties cards, all glossy in black and white

18

with just a splash of scarlet. Eventually we compromised with a delicious Tissot boating scene and made our way out into the street.

'Now then,' I said, 'where shall we go?'

'Oh, do you think we might go to Baxter's? It's where we always used to go with your dear mother in the old days, when we used to meet out shopping. I haven't been there for ages. Thelma likes that new place in Fore Street— she says that the stairs at Baxter's would be too much for me, but I'm *sure* I can manage them if you lend me your arm, dear, and we take it slowly.'

We negotiated the stairs successfully and found a table by the window, just as we always used to do.

'I remember once,' Mrs Rossiter said, 'when you were such a little mite, you sat under the table and wouldn't come out. Your poor mother was quite in despair. But you whispered to me that you were being a bear in a cave so *I* said that bears always came out of their caves for buns, and I got the waitress to bring you one of those very sugary buns and so you came out. Do you remember?'

Fortunately I am now of an age when I am no longer embarrassed by such revelations of childhood misdemeanours, only touched that anyone, outside the family, should remember them affectionately after all this time.

'How extraordinary that you should remember that!' I said. 'I was a tiresome child,

19

I'm afraid. An only child, too much with adults—that's what Mrs Dudley used to tell Mother!'

'That woman!' Mrs Rossiter almost snorted. 'Bone selfish and always has been. How she managed to have two such nice children as Rosemary and Martin I shall never know—*and* she still leads them a terrible dance. How anyone who loved her children could be so selfish and demanding! Of course, now Martin's gone to live in Doncaster it all falls on poor Rosemary. That woman is a saint! She waits on her mother hand, foot and finger.'

'I know,' I said, 'it's really awful.' Rosemary is my best friend and I do worry at the way her horrible old mother is wearing her out.

The waitress came to take our order and I said, 'Shall we have some of those sugary buns with our coffee?'

Her eyes lit up like a child offered a treat.

'Oh yes, let's!'

We chatted about happy times in the past—mostly very simple things, and I felt how sad it was that someone who had had every material advantage and comfort should cling in her memory to the relatively few moments of warmth and affection that Mother and I had been able to give her.

I walked back with her through Jubilee Gardens and we both exclaimed at the beauty of the almond and the winter cherry blossom.

'I do thank God every year,' she said, 'that

I've lived to see another spring.'

'Oh yes,' I said, 'like the Housman poem—

"Fifty years is little room
To look at cherry trees in bloom."

'I think that wasting your life is the worst crime, really,' she said thoughtfully. 'Worse than suicide, even.'

I was startled. 'But you,' I said, 'you haven't wasted *your* life. You ran that great big house, you did a lot for the county—all that voluntary work—you brought up Alan and Thelma...'

My voice died away. I couldn't quite bring myself to mention Colonel Rossiter.

'Yes, of course, you're right, dear, I've had a very full life.' Her voice was brisk. 'Don't take any notice of me—it's the spring, I expect!'

We got to the door of West Lodge and I hugged her in farewell, but she didn't go in.

'I think I'll just go for a little stroll along the sea-front before lunch,' she said. 'Take care of yourself and give my love to Michael. How lucky you are to have that dear boy. It would have been lovely to have a grandchild—but, of course, with the business—well, Thelma had to make a choice and I do quite understand. God bless you, my dear.'

She walked round the corner and crossed over to the promenade and I watched the slight figure slowly moving along towards the harbour, occasionally stopping to look at the

21

gulls wheeling and swooping along the foreshore.

I suddenly remembered that I hadn't returned my library books so I turned back into the town. I was standing by the trolley of returned books hoping, as I always did, that the fact that other people had just been reading them might make them, somehow, more desirable, when an arm reached past me to snatch up a Catherine Cookson. I turned, half in protest at being jostled, and saw that the eager reader was Annie Fisher.

'Hello, Annie,' I said, 'how's the world treating you?'

'Oh, Mrs Malory—mustn't grumble, I suppose. But I'm glad the year's on the turn—I don't like the winter and that's a fact.'

'Yes, well, we've got the spring to look forward to now,' I said. Then, to make conversation, I went on, 'I've just been having coffee with Mrs Rossiter. I met her in Smiths.'

'She's never been let out, has she? That's really criminal. Poor lady, she's been really poorly. That Mrs Wilmot—calls herself a matron—no idea of looking after old people. They need keeping warm and resting. Mrs Rossiter should still be in her bed, not gallivanting all over the town!'

She appeared to be quite upset and I hastened to reassure her.

'She seemed all right to me,' I said. 'A bit thin, of course, but that's only to be expected

22

after she's been ill. She was in very good spirits—we went to Baxter's.'

'You never made her go up all those stairs?' Annie's sharp little face glared up at me so fiercely that I felt guilty and uncomfortable. 'Not with her heart being like it is!'

'We took them very slowly, Annie, and she did enjoy going there again.'

'Well, it's to be hoped that she went straight back and had a nice lie down.'

I refrained from telling her about Mrs Rossiter's walk along the sea-front. I tried to remember if Annie had always been as over-protective of her mistress in the old days but, of course, when Colonel Rossiter had been alive she had been very firmly kept in her place. To change the subject I asked if she had any news of her brother in Australia. She became quite animated.

'Well, fancy you asking me that, Mrs Malory! I had a letter from Sam only this morning. He says he's coming over next month—isn't that wonderful? I know Mrs Rossiter will be so pleased to see him again. It'll be just like the old days.'

I must have looked puzzled for she said impatiently, 'Sam used to be gardener up at the Manor before he went away.'

'Yes, of course, I remember now.'

My memories of Sam Fisher were of a rather disagreeable man, lazy and (when he had the opportunity) dishonest. Colonel Rossiter had

23

eventually dismissed him—not for either of these faults but because once, after spending a rather long lunch-hour in the local pub, Sam Fisher had been 'insubordinate'. Annie appeared to have forgotten the circumstances of her brother's departure from the Manor and seemed genuinely pleased at the thought of reuniting, as she saw it, two old friends.

'That *will* be nice for you,' I said, with that sort of over-emphatic warmth that we use when we are not quite sincere. 'And I believe you told me that he's been doing very well in Australia. It must be a beautiful country. Does he have a family over there?'

A shadow crossed her face. 'His wife went off and left him a couple of years ago and took their daughter with her. I've never seen my niece, only photos. But he's well rid of his wife—a flighty piece from what I've heard. Sam's always been respectable, like me. Yes, he's done very well for himself. Got his own business, a garage—always been good with his hands, well, you remember that. And, then, of course, there's the Church...'

It seemed that Sam Fisher was a born-again something or other. She went on at some length about his standing in the local community and this rather evangelical church. I let the words flow over me as I so often did when Annie was in full flood and made polite murmuring noises that seemed to satisfy her.

'I'll pop down and see Mrs Rossiter this

afternoon,' she said, 'and give her the good news. Sam said he'd be hiring a car while he's here so we can take her for a drive up over the hill. Have a nice cream tea out somewhere.'

'I'm sure she'd like that,' I said, feeling once more a touch of guilt that it was Annie, who had so little, who was going to give Mrs Rossiter this treat and not I, who had so much. Perhaps the same thoughts were going through Annie's mind, for she gave a small nod of satisfaction.

'Well, I must be getting on,' she said. 'Can't stand here talking all day.'

She moved over to the counter with her Catherine Cookson and I went rather morosely to scan once more the biography shelves in case something exciting had materialised in the last five minutes.

Later, as I was cutting up some heart for the animals, I tried to analyse just why I disliked Annie so much.

'I suppose it's her manner, really,' I told Foss, who was weaving round my ankles, uttering low meat-demanding cries. 'I'm sure she has a heart of gold and she is truly devoted to Mrs Rossiter. It's just that she always seems to put me in the wrong—as if there's some lack of consideration in me. I suppose I'm the selfish one—just wanting poor Mrs Rossiter to be there when I feel like going to see her, but not every day, like Annie. I expect Mrs Rossiter has left her something in her will. I don't suppose Thelma would do anything for her—too fond of money on her own account.'

I broke off and gave a sudden cry. Foss had stopped weaving and, impatient with my dilatoriness, had jumped on to my shoulder (with his claws out to help him balance) to get a closer view of the food. I lifted him carefully off and rubbed my shoulder ruefully.

'All right,' I said, 'I'll get on with the matter in hand.'

*   *   *

A few days later I picked a large bunch of primroses and a few violets (I know they never last in water but I couldn't resist their delicate mauve faces) and took them along to West Lodge for Mrs Rossiter. In the entrance hall I met Mrs Wilmot, the Matron, who greeted me effusively.

'And who's the lucky person who's going to have those beautiful flowers? Such a lovely posy, quite like a painting!'

'They're for Mrs Rossiter, actually.'

'Well now, she *has* got a visitor—but, of course, you are old friends, aren't you? It's Mrs Douglas, her daughter. What a nice surprise for you! She told me that it's her mother's birthday this week and she always likes to come down to see her round about then. Isn't that nice! But, of course, I don't have to tell you, Mrs Malory, how thoughtful Mrs

Douglas is and how good she's always been to her mother—not like some I could mention. The tales I could tell you! It takes all sorts, I suppose. Still, it *is* so nice to see a daughter so devoted to her mother. Quite restores one's faith in human nature, you might say.'

I gave Mrs Wilmot a brief, false smile and made my way up to Mrs Rossiter's room. It was Thelma's voice that called out 'Come in' in response to my knock and it was Thelma who took the bunch of primroses from my hand.

'Look, Mummy, at the lovely flowers that Sheila has brought you—*isn't* that kind of her?'

I felt cheated. I had wanted to put the flowers into Mrs Rossiter's hand and see her eyes light up as they always did when I brought her some small remembrance. She was pleased, of course, but gave only a polite little murmur and a shy smile.

'I know how you love primroses,' I said, hearing my voice sound too emphatic. Thelma Douglas is one of those small, slim, energetic women who make me feel like a large, ponderous, slow-thinking, unfashionable provincial. From her neat dark head (untouched by grey) to her small feet in their ridiculously high-heeled shoes she epitomised everything that was urban and elegant. It is an extraordinary paradox, I suppose, that one should feel inferior to people one really despises. Not for one moment would I ever want to be like Thelma—but still, I couldn't help wishing that I wasn't wearing an old camel jacket and a tweed skirt—both embellished with dog-hairs—and a pair of flat, comfortable shoes.

Thelma came back from the bathroom with a vase full of water and picked up the primroses.

'*Aren't* they lovely! I adore the spring, such an exciting time of the year!'

She tucked the primroses neatly into the vase, pausing when she had finished with the violets in her hand.

'I'm afraid these won't go in properly. I always think it's such a pity to *pick* them really—they never last in water.'

Mrs Rossiter got up from her chair and quickly took the violets from her daughter.

'They're so beautiful. Look, I've got this tiny glass vase—they'll just fit nicely. And did you know,' she smiled at me, 'they drink through their faces, so if you turn them upside down at night they last for days!'

Thelma laughed. 'What extraordinary things you know about, Mummy,' she said. And, turning to me, 'Now do tell me what you've been doing—all the gossip in the town. I always think that real life is lived here and not in London!'

This was so palpably untrue that I didn't even bother to reply, but said, 'Oh, nothing ever happens here—what about you? How is Gordon? Your mother tells me that the

28

business is doing splendidly, you must both be so busy.'

'My dear, it's frantic, just a madhouse from morning to night. But so *stimulating*—I do feel my brain would *atrophy* if I didn't have at least half a dozen problems to be solved every day! But yes'—she lowered her voice as she prepared to talk seriously about the one thing that really mattered to her—'the business is doing very well indeed. We have these two new accounts.' She mentioned brand names that we had heard of even down in Taviscombe.

'Goodness,' I said, impressed in spite of myself, 'you must be doing well.'

'We're at a tricky stage, of course. We ought to be expanding to take advantage of big accounts like those—new offices, bigger staff—but there's a cash-flow problem. When is there not? But it's a difficult time to raise the finance, as you can imagine, with the City being a bit jumpy and 1992 almost upon us.'

She held forth for some little time on this theme and then, as if deciding that it was probably all above my head, she said, 'But I expect all this seems dreadfully mundane to an intellectual like you.'

The fact that I have written some articles and a few books of literary criticism always made Thelma refer to me in this (to me) repellent way. But I was used to it by now and no longer protested.

'I think it all sounds quite fascinating,' I

said, 'and I shall expect to be invited to the party when you and Gordon make your *second* million!'

She laughed again but looked, I thought, complacent.

'What about tea?' she said, and rang the bell. Amazingly quickly a cheerful woman in a green overall appeared.

'Oh, Ivy,' Mrs Rossiter said, 'can you manage tea for my daughter and for Mrs Malory?'

'Oh yes, Mrs Rossiter, right away.' She turned to me. 'Nice to see you, Mrs Malory. How's Mr Michael getting on then in London?'

'Oh, he's having a lovely time, thank you, Ivy. I'll tell him you were asking for him.'

'Ivy used to work for my mother,' I explained to Thelma's raised eyebrows when Ivy had gone.

'Oh, I see. And how *is* Michael? I hadn't realised that he was living in London.'

'He's at the College of Law,' I said.

'Oh, so he's going to be a solicitor is he, like his father? There's a lot of money in the law nowadays. I know for a fact that some of the City solicitors—tax experts and so forth—are making six-figure salaries.'

'I don't think Michael wants to work in London. I think he'd quite like to come back to Taviscombe.'

'Oh, that would be *such* a mistake. Of

course, he's fond of you, but it never works, you know, keeping them tied to your apron-strings.'

I bit back a furious denial and only said quite mildly that Michael would doubtless make up his own mind when he'd finished his two-year course.

Ivy returned with the tea and I was amused to see that the tray bore a tea-pot and full tea-set, not just the single cups that usually appeared, also slices of fruit cake and a rather superior kind of biscuit. I thought I detected the hand of Mrs Wilmot. Thelma poured.

Over tea Thelma's monologue continued and I realised that I was not going to have an opportunity for any sort of conversation with Mrs Rossiter. When I had had a cup of tea, I got up to leave. 'It's been lovely seeing you, Thelma, and hearing all about how you're getting on, but I must leave you to have a chat with your mother. You've come all this way . . .'

Mrs Rossiter smiled at me and squeezed my hand. 'The flowers are really beautiful,' she said. 'Come again soon.'

Thelma stood up. 'I'll just come with you to your car.' As we walked along the corridor and down the stairs she chatted vivaciously about life in London—the latest musical, the newest fashionable restaurant, which television actors they were using in their commercials. In the hall Mrs Wilmot, who was hovering near the front door, came over.

'Oh, Mrs Douglas, you're not going yet, are you?'

'No, I'm just saying goodbye to Mrs Malory. I'll have a word with you before I go.'

She gave a little nod of dismissal and Mrs Wilmot drifted away, giving me a vague smile of recognition. Outside Thelma sat down on one of the benches, empty for the moment since their usual elderly occupants, who spent many long hours watching for any sort of activity on the sea-front, were all indoors having tea.

'Can you spare a minute, Sheila? I just wanted to have a word about Mummy.'

'Yes, of course.' I sat down beside her.

'How do you think she's looking?'

'Well, she's still not quite herself,' I said cautiously, 'after that bout of flu, but she seems very spry to me. What do you think?'

'Well, to be honest, Sheila, I'm really rather worried about her. You know I always want to do what's best for her; that's why I persuaded her to move out of the Manor. It really was too much for her. And she seems very happy at West Lodge.'

This was a statement rather than a question and something impelled me to say, 'I know she couldn't stay at the Manor but it seems a pity, when she's so active, that she couldn't have just taken a flat in Taviscombe or something. I'm sure Annie Fisher would have been happy to go on looking after her.'

An expression of distaste crossed her face. 'Oh no, that wouldn't have done at all. Annie was getting far too familiar—a very encroaching type of woman. It simply wouldn't have answered. West Lodge is the best place for Mummy now. She's settled in beautifully and has made lots of friends.'

I looked at her enquiringly and she said impatiently, 'Oh, that Polish woman—I can never remember her name—and I'm sure there are plenty of others. They seem a very jolly crowd there.'

The inappropriateness of this phrase in relation to West Lodge stunned me into silence.

'I worry so much less,' she continued, 'now that I know she is somewhere *safe* where she can be looked after properly. Of course, you were so *lucky* being able to look after your mother at home. You don't know how difficult it is, Sheila, to look after things from a distance. The responsibility is so much greater—one is always on *edge* wondering how things are going.'

My mother had been an invalid for many years and I had indeed been lucky to have a loving husband who insisted that she made her home with us. I was lucky, too, that I had been able to have the kind of career (if career it could be called) that could be pursued from home. Still, I rather resented Thelma's bland assumption that it had all been so easy. Also I was pretty sure that as soon as Thelma was on the train to Paddington (first class, tax deductible) she dismissed her mother from her mind.

'Anyway,' she said, 'I really am worried about her. She looks *very* frail. I'm sure she's lost a lot of weight, although I believe the food at West Lodge is excellent. And, of course, there's the angina. I know Dr Moore is *most* concerned about her.'

'But I thought he said that it was only a mild condition and that she'd be fine if she didn't do anything too strenuous. At least, that's what she told me.'

'Isn't that like her? Always making light of things. But I assure you that it really is serious—she could go at any time. Or at least, she might have to be moved to a hospital at a moment's notice. And have you noticed how she can't remember things from one minute to the next?'

'Well, no, I haven't. She always seems to me to be very much on the ball! I only wish I were half as alert as she is. My memory's shocking these days. Do you know, I often have to go all the way downstairs and come back up again just to remember what I went upstairs for in the first place!'

Thelma seemed uninterested in my problems. 'Of course she always has been very vague.'

'Oh, not *vague*,' I protested.

Thelma ignored my interruption. 'And you know how these things get worse in old age. I don't say that she's actually *senile*...'

'Oh, for goodness' sake!'

'Well, not yet, but as she gets older it's going to get more difficult. There is, you know, a great deal of money involved.' There was real concern in her voice now. 'Things were left in a very unsatisfactory way when Daddy died. There was this stupid Trust—something my grandfather set up—and, as things stand, Mummy and her sister Maud have control of what amounts to a small fortune!'

'Well,' I said provocatively, 'it's marvellous to think that your mother needn't worry about money. I know West Lodge is frightfully expensive.'

'Yes, of course.' Thelma brushed this consideration aside. 'But you see if she should get really senile, then it would be very difficult. That's why I want her to give me power of attorney.'

So that was why Thelma had paid a birthday visit to her mother.

'Have you mentioned it to her yet?' I asked.

'Yes, today. But she's being rather silly about it. I mean, it's for *her* sake; I'm not trying to *swindle* her out of her inheritance or anything. After all, I *am* her daughter!'

'So what did she say?'

'That she'd have to think about it and talk to Mr Robertson. That stupid old fool—do you

35

know he doesn't even have a computer in that dreary Dickensian office of his! I can imagine what *his* advice would be!'

'What does Alan think?'

'Oh, Alan!' she said impatiently. 'He's no use. I tried to ring him at that Ecology Centre of his—it's somewhere near Harare—but they said he was on his way back to England for some conference or other. Anyway, he's not *here*, he hasn't got to cope. Typical of him to go swanning around the world and leave me to do everything for Mummy. He just about sends her a card for Christmas and that's all! Gordon thinks I'm absolutely right—you know what a good business head he has and we've got Simon (he's our lawyer and an absolute charmer!) to do the paperwork. All she has to do is sign.'

'I can see how she would feel,' I said. 'I suppose we would all like to look after our own affairs while we can.'

'But that's so *selfish*,' Thelma said vehemently. 'It will just leave us with a dreadful mess to clear up after she's gone. Look, Sheila'—she lowered her voice persuasively—'she thinks a lot of you. I'm sure you could persuade her—that it's all for her own good. You really would be *helping* her in the long run, and I know you've always been fond of her.'

I was amazed and horrified and said rather formally, 'I don't think I could do that, Thelma. It's something she must decide for

36

herself.'

She was obviously furious with me and, remembering how she used to vent her temper when she was a child by pinching my arm, I instinctively drew away from her. Controlling herself, she smiled at me and said, 'Well, if she *does* discuss the matter with you, do try and make her see sense.'

She got up abruptly from the seat. 'I must get back. I want to have a word with Mrs Wilmot before I go and I've got a taxi coming at four thirty. I *must* get the five thirty-five from Taunton—we're having dinner with some clients at the Dorchester this evening and it's going to be a hellish rush. Still'—she gave me her rather saccharine smile—'I simply *had* to pop down for a birthday visit.'

'I'm sure she appreciates it,' I said, getting up (rather more stiffly than Thelma). 'It was a lovely surprise to see you. Please give my regards to Gordon.'

She gave me the smile again and a little wave and went back into West Lodge. I had left my car up by the harbour and was walking towards it when I ran into my friend Rosemary. Well, actually, she nearly ran into me since she was being pulled along by two large dogs, her own black labrador and a brindled boxer which belonged to her daughter Jilly.

'Oh, Sheila, I wanted to have a word about the Red Cross Bring and Buy. Can you come along while I just put these two in the car? I can't possibly talk while they're rushing along like this. Dusky's fine on her own, but Alpha simply eggs her on. Do you know what the little monster did yesterday? She ate a whole hairbrush, bristles and all! I was frantic—I rushed her round to the vet—just left the supper to burn on the stove—but he said she was all right.'

'She certainly looks all right now,' I said, as Alpha leaped up at me and tried to lick my face lovingly. Dusky rushed round in circles barking her approval and winding the leads around Rosemary's legs.

'Here,' I said, 'you give me Alpha's lead.'

Somehow we got to Rosemary's car and bundled them into the back.

'Goodness!' Rosemary slammed the door on them quickly. 'They're so strong.'

After clambering back and forth across the front seats they suddenly collapsed on top of each other and went to sleep.

'Do I gather that Jilly and Roger are away?' I asked.

'Yes. The baby's due quite soon now so they thought perhaps a long weekend while they still can.'

'You could have done without Alpha just now,' I said.

Rosemary's mother had just had a slight stroke. With her iron constitution she had got over the effects very quickly, but she had seized the opportunity to tighten her hold over poor Rosemary, whom she kept running around obeying a multiplicity of largely contradictory commands.

'Well, she is being particularly awkward at the moment. She's decided she wants a stair-lift put in. She's never thought of it before but apparently a crony of hers has got one and told her that you can get a grant for it. You can imagine the chaos *that* will cause!'

Mrs Dudley, though well off, was not one to pass up anything that might be going free, whether she really wanted it or not.

'And, of course,' Rosemary went on, 'there's no hope that she'll let me deal with it; you know how she always insists on doing everything in her own way. She'll get the cheapest possible builder—actually there aren't many left in Taviscombe that she hasn't quarrelled with—and the job will be done badly and I'll have to clear up the mess because by then she'll have convinced herself that it was all my fault in the first place.'

'If there was any justice,' I said viciously, 'she'd fall off the wretched thing and break her neck!'

Rosemary giggled. 'Not with my luck. She'd just fracture a wrist or something and need *constant* attention. I wouldn't mind if she'd just occasionally say thank you or make some sign of appreciation, but she's always going on about how nobody ever does anything for her.

She was furious when Jilly and Roger left Alpha with me.'

'I can imagine,' I said. 'She said that you were looking very tired and that you did too much for other people.'

'How did you guess!'

'Talking of doing things,' I said, 'what about the Red Cross thing?'

'Oh, yes. We can't have the Church Hall that day, so we must either change the date—and you remember what hell it was trying to get a time that suited everyone—or we must find somewhere else.'

'Oh, Lord! I suppose we should have booked it ages in advance. Spring Fayres proliferate almost as much as Christmas Fêtes nowadays. What about the Methodist Hall in Harbour Road?'

'No good—they've got the Ramblers' AGM.'

'Oh, for goodness' sake, why aren't they out rambling instead of cluttering up the only other possible hall! Leave it with me and I'll see if I can persuade the Hon. Liz to let us have it at the Dower House. We'd probably get a better crowd there—people always like to go and gawp.'

The Honourable Elizabeth Clough was the relict of our local lord of the manor and could sometimes be bullied—or flattered—into letting us hold the occasional event in the great hall of her stately home.

40

'Oh, bless you, Sheila, that *would* be a weight off my mind. I wish to God I could get Mother to go into West Lodge for a couple weeks, just till after the baby's born. I do want to be with Jilly then. But you know how stubborn she is.'

'I went to West Lodge today,' I said, 'to see Mrs Rossiter. And guess what, Horrible Thelma was there.'

Rosemary pulled a face. 'I haven't seen her for ages. Is she as Horrible as ever?'

'Oh, worse. Poor Mrs Rossiter—Thelma's trying to make her sign a power of attorney.'

'Well, I suppose it might be easier, with Thelma so far away. If anything happened, I mean.'

'If it was anyone else but Thelma I might agree, but I'm sure she's got her beady little eyes fixed on that money. There's rather a lot, you know. And I think she's cooking something up with Gordon and their solicitor. Anyway, Mrs Rossiter seems perfectly healthy to me. At least she didn't give in to Thelma straight away. She said she'd have to consult Arthur Robertson.'

'Well, I wouldn't give much for her chances of holding out if Thelma has made up her mind. Mrs R. is sweet but people have been bossing her around and pushing her aside all her life. Remember those dreadful parties!'

Rosemary had been forced to go to Thelma's birthday parties because Mrs Dudley, who was a dreadful old snob, would never have let her

41

daughter refuse an invitation from a child whose mother was rich, whose father had aristocratic connections and who lived in a Manor. We used to hate the stiff formality, which the over-lavish food and expensive entertainer did little to alleviate. Colonel Rossiter would invariably be present, falsely genial, and then there was Thelma herself, with her sharp-eyed evaluation of the proffered birthday present, which always seemed inadequate as she unwrapped it and cast it aside with perfunctory thanks. Worst of all—to me at any rate—was the sight of poor Mrs Rossiter, trying so hard to make things comfortable and pleasant for the young guests (she was genuinely fond of children and left to herself got on well with them) and being snubbed and scornfully disregarded by her daughter and her husband.

'Goodness, yes, weren't they *dire*? Do you remember that year when the conjurer didn't show up and Colonel Rossiter blamed her and went storming out—and Thelma went up to her room in a sulk. Actually, though, it was the nicest party of all, because Mrs Rossiter organised silly games like pass the parcel and musical chairs and we all had a marvellous time until Thelma heard us enjoying ourselves and came downstairs and cast a blight on the whole affair.'

Rosemary suddenly looked at her watch. 'Oh Lord, I've got to go. I've got Mother's salmon for her supper and I must get it back so that Elsie can cook it for her before she goes. Mother won't let me do it, thank goodness, she says I dry it up!'

She wrenched open the car door, quelled the excited dogs and drove away.

I stood for a moment pondering on the unfairness of life that gave Rosemary a mother like Mrs Dudley and Thelma one like Mrs Rossiter. What a pity we couldn't choose our parents. But then, I wondered, what about our own children—would they choose us?

This seemed an unprofitable and even disquieting matter for speculation so I sensibly went home to cook my own less exciting supper.

CHAPTER THREE

'Is something *wrong* with Mrs Rossiter,' Mrs Jankiewicz said. 'I do not know what it is for she does not tell me, but is something.'

'I suppose it does take a little while to settle in a new place,' I replied, 'especially somewhere like West Lodge when you've been used to living in a large house with lots of space.'

'Is not that,' she said positively, 'she does not worry about such things—she was glad to leave that gloomy house, I think. No, is

43

something that has happen, I am sure. I notice a difference in her. She is so sad all the time and there is something on her mind. She come for a tea last week because it is my names day. Was not a tea like *we* used to have, do you remember?'

'No small fish?' I laughed.

I used to go to tea with Sophie, when we were both at school, and I was always enchanted by the novelty and foreignness of the food. There was Polish ham and the 'small fish'—a kind of especially delicious sardine—wonderful cheesecake and delicate, airy cinnamon biscuits covered in icing sugar. And tea, of course, from the silver samovar.

'I get the girl here to fetch me some cheesecake, but is not the same, like I make.'

'Oh that was wonderful. And that lovely one you used to do—sponge with those little dark plums! Do you know, I still use your recipe for bigos—so wonderfully warm and comforting in the winter—Michael loves it!'

Mrs Jankiewicz smiled and I led her back into the past and let her tell me once again about the picnics they had on her grandmother's estate in Eastern Poland when she was a girl. But the memory of what she said about Mrs Rossiter stayed with me and nagged away in my mind. I felt I ought to go and see her and find out what the trouble was, but she was such a private person and I didn't want her to think that I was interfering, or that Mrs

Jankiewicz and I had been talking about her behind her back.

* * *

About a week later I was walking through Jubilee Gardens when I saw Mrs Rossiter sitting on one of the benches. This was unusual since, unlike most of the residents of West Lodge, she preferred to go further afield. She was sitting quite still with her hands resting in her lap and her face raised to catch the warmth of the sun, but she didn't really looked relaxed and peaceful, although it was a beautiful spring afternoon and the flower beds around her were brilliant with wallflowers and forget-me-nots. Watching her from a distance I was struck by the great sadness of her expression, almost a sort of hopelessness.

I drew level with her and called out a greeting. She turned her head and, just for a moment, didn't seem to recognise me. I was alarmed and wondered if perhaps Thelma had been right about her mother's failing capabilities. But then she smiled and said quite normally, 'Sheila, dear, how nice to see you.'

I sat down on the seat beside her and commented on the beauty of the day. 'And aren't the flowers lovely this year? The colours seem richer than usual. Perhaps it's because we had such a mild winter. Look at those wallflowers—did you ever see such colours?'

She turned to look at them. 'When I was a girl, my mother always used to call them gilly-flowers. Of course, we couldn't grow them out in Africa. We had all sorts of exotic lilies and things, but it was the English flowers my mother missed—the gilly-flowers, the primroses and the bluebells. When Maud and I were children she used to tell us how they always used to decorate the church at Easter with masses of primroses—they went out the day before into the woods to pick them and tied them up in bunches with wool, so as not to bruise the stems. We loved to hear about England. Poor Maud,' she sighed. 'She's in a bad way now, I'm afraid. Marion, her daughter—you remember her, she married a Dutchman—says it's only a matter of time. But Thelma doesn't think I should make the journey up to Scotland to see her. And, if I did go up there, what could I say? We were never very close. We write occasionally, but after we came back to England we drifted apart; we haven't seen each other for years. All we have in common now, I suppose, is our childhood in Africa.'

'I'd forgotten that you were brought up in South Africa.'

'Yes, just outside Durban. Of course it was very different then.'

'Do you ever feel you'd like to go back and see it all again?'

'It wouldn't be as I remember it and there are

46

too many memories. I don't think I would like to see it now.'

'That's what Mrs Jankiewicz says. She says that the Poland she knew has gone and even now, under the new régime, she wouldn't want to go back and overlay her memories with something new and alien.'

'Memories are the most important things we have when we grow old,' Mrs Rossiter said. 'We must treat them with care so that they will last out our lives.'

She spoke very positively in a reflective, almost melancholy tone, quite unlike her usual shy, hesitant manner.

'Yes, I know,' I said, 'I've felt that such a lot lately, since Peter and Mother died. Keeping my memories of them fresh so that they don't somehow slip away from me as time goes by. Sometimes I get into a panic because I can't remember what their voices sounded like...'

'It doesn't matter about the voices, as long as you remember what they said.'

We sat in silence for a while and then I said, 'It was nice to see Thelma again. It must have been a lovely surprise for you when she turned up last week.'

'Yes,' she said, 'it was a surprise.'

'I thought she was looking marvellous.' I tried to put a little enthusiasm into my voice.

'Thelma does look very smart,' she replied. 'She always cared a great deal about her appearance, even as a little girl.'

'I gather that the business is doing very well.'

'So she tells me. She and Gordon certainly work very hard.'

From her rather forced replies to my remarks, I gathered that she was still unhappy about Thelma's proposal of a power of attorney. I wondered if she might mention it to me but she changed the subject to Mrs Jankiewicz's arthritis and how she was finding it increasingly difficult to get about.

'Poor soul—it must be terrible never to be able to get out of that place.'

'West Lodge?' I was surprised to hear her refer to it so vehemently.

'Never to get out and feel the air on your face or smell the sea!'

'You're right, of course. I must try and get her out for a drive while the weather's still nice. I feel very guilty that I've neglected her a bit these last few weeks.'

'No, my dear, you mustn't feel guilty. You lead such a busy life—all those good works. And then there's your writing, not to mention Michael.'

We talked for a little while about Mrs Jankiewicz, but I felt that I didn't have her full attention and that she had a problem on her mind that she had come out into Jubilee Gardens to think over. I got to my feet.

'Are you going in for tea?'

'No, dear, I think I'll just sit here for a bit while the sun is still nice.'

'If you're sure, then.'

I gave her a brief hug and she clung to me for a moment, then patted my arm. 'You're a good girl, Sheila. Thank you for all your kindness.'

I felt tears pricking my eyes at this undeserved praise and, with an inarticulate murmur, I went on my way.

I took Mrs Jankiewicz for her drive and it was a great success, for, although she couldn't see much of the countryside, she did enjoy standing on the high moor and smelling, as she said, spring in the air. Also she was able to give me a blow by blow description of her encounter with Mr Williams's son and how she had Given Him a Piece of Her Mind—the recounting of which triumph gave her great pleasure and me considerable amusement.

'I have to go to London for several weeks,' I said, 'to do some research in the British Library, but I'll be in to see you when I get back. Could you keep a special eye on Mrs Rossiter while I'm away? I'm not very happy about her.'

'Ever since that Thelma came,' Mrs Jankiewicz said with her usual perception, 'she is sad and troubled. Is a hard one that daughter, no love for her mother, only show. And the son, so far away, and never writes— not like my Zofia.'

She pulled an airmail letter from the huge black handbag in which she carried a large proportion of her more portable possessions.

49

'Read,' she said. 'Adam is coming to study at Cambridge. He is a clever boy, like his grandfather. He will come to see his old grandmother very often.'

I reflected that Sophie's life wouldn't be worth living if he didn't.

'Perhaps he could come and stay with us for a few days while Michael's home. They used to play together when they were small children, before Sophie went to Canada.'

'Perhaps,' Mrs Jankiewicz said mournfully, 'brought up in that country he will be like those gangsters on TV, driving the cars too fast and carrying a gun!'

'Oh I don't think Canada's like that,' I said. 'And most of those television gangster films are set in London now. Anyway, Sophie and Taddeus will have brought him up properly— you can be sure of that.'

I poured us both some more tea from the flask and Mrs Jankiewicz said suddenly, 'She is not taking her sleeping tablets.'

'Sleeping tablets?' I echoed, thoroughly confused.

'Mrs Rossiter.'

After the manner of their generation they were always Mrs Rossiter and Mrs Jankiewicz to each other, not Edith and Jadwiga.

'How do you know?'

'Last week I was in her room and she opened a drawer in her desk and I saw a number of them—they are the same like I have, black and green. Were sleeping tablets.'

'Did you say anything?' I asked.

'Is her business if she does not want to take the drugs they give her. I do not blame her. In these places they try to destroy your will and take away your independence.'

This was spoken so vehemently—fiercely even—and Mrs Jankiewicz, in spite of her age and infirmities, looked so full of will-power and independence that I couldn't help laughing. After a moment she gave a reluctant smile.

'No. Not me, perhaps, thanks God. But poor Mrs Rossiter, who has never had a will of her own—soon she is just a vegetable, sitting all day long in her room like the other vegetables there. That is what her daughter want, I am sure.'

I was pretty sure, too, but thought it better not to say so.

'Do have another cake,' I said. 'I know you like these almond ones.'

That evening I found my mind going back to Mrs Jankiewicz's words. I supposed that there was no reason why Mrs Rossiter should have taken her sleeping tablets if she felt she didn't need them, but I was uneasy at the thought of that little cache of tablets in her desk drawer.

*   *   *

When I got back from London the roses were

out in the formal beds outside West Lodge and spring had, in the way that it does, imperceptibly turned into summer. As I went into the hall I was stopped by Mrs Wilmot, whose usual bland manner seemed to have deserted her. Indeed she was positively agitated.

'Oh, Mrs Malory, I'm so glad you've come—I've been trying to get hold of you for several days now.'

'I've been away,' I explained. 'Why, whatever's happened?'

'Have you heard from Mrs Rossiter at all?'

'Mrs Rossiter? No—I've just called in today to see her. And Mrs Jankiewicz, too; my usual round, in fact.'

She dismissed my little pleasantry impatiently.

'She's not here. She went off on Tuesday and hasn't come back.'

'Tuesday—but that's three days ago!'

'You can imagine how worried we are.'

'What happened?'

An elderly man leaning heavily on his walking frame came shuffling towards us.

'We can't talk about it here,' Mrs Wilmot said. 'Come into my office.'

Mrs Wilmot's office was not so much a place of business as a replica of an Edwardian drawing room with white panelled walls, gilt-framed watercolours, glass-fronted cabinets full of china and a general impression of

52

chintz-covered chairs and tiny rosewood tables. The idea, I suppose, was to create an illusion of gracious living for the relatives of prospective residents. She waved me to a seat on one of the sofas and sat down herself in a high-backed winged armchair, giving a despairing sigh.

'Oh dear, if you haven't heard anything ... You were my last hope.'

'But how did it happen? I mean, how did she go?'

'It was Tuesday, my busiest day. Dr Randall comes that day to see some of his patients and you know how difficult—that is, how *fussy* he can be! *And* it's the laundry day and the day the chiropodist comes too. Well, as you can imagine I was on the go all morning, so I didn't actually see her leave. I knew she was going to take a taxi into Taunton and do some shopping that day—she does sometimes, you know, it makes a nice little break for her. I mean, she's really quite active for her age and quite capable of a little trip like that, whatever her daughter may say.'

She sounded defensive and I imagined that Thelma must have been very forthright indeed about her lack of supervision of Mrs Rossiter, so I said soothingly, 'Oh, yes, she is. Mrs Rossiter is perfectly all right on her own, and she does enjoy little outings like that so much.'

Mrs Wilmot was apparently heartened by this support. 'It seems she couldn't get her usual taxi (she rang through herself) but Ivy recognised the man—I think she said his name was Ed Cooper—when she went to see Mrs Rossiter off.'

'Oh, she actually saw her go?'

'Oh, yes. And she had just her handbag and shopping bag, nothing else. She said to Ivy that she'd probably be back for tea and that was the last any of us saw of her.'

'Good heavens! What an extraordinary thing.'

'Of course, when she hadn't come back for dinner—the residents have their dinner at six o'clock sharp—Ivy came and told me and I rang round all the hospitals. I really was quite dreadfully worried. Then, when the time went on, at about eight o'clock, I telephoned the police.'

'And what did they say?'

'Well, what *could* they say! They were as baffled as I was. We rang Mrs Douglas—you can imagine how upset she was—but Mrs Rossiter wasn't with her.'

'Have you tried Annie Fisher? She used to work for Mrs Rossiter and often came to visit her here.'

'Mrs Douglas suggested that and gave me her address—one of those council flats down by the marshes—and I've telephoned several times but there's no reply, so she must be away. So that's no good.'

We sat in silence as I tried to gather my

thoughts. I simply couldn't believe that Mrs Rossiter had gone. And without telling anyone. It was totally unlike her; she was so punctilious in her dealings with other people, she would never have simply gone off without letting anyone know where she was. I couldn't think of anything to say, so I just sat there and looked about me. Was that rather splendid silhouette of a Regency gentleman with a pronounced Roman nose one of Mrs Wilmot's ancestors, I wondered? Or was he part of the carefully arranged décor? I suspected the latter. Mrs Wilmot was the sort of person whom it was impossible to imagine as a child or, indeed, with a family of any kind; she seemed to exist only at the particular moment and in the particular place where one was accustomed to see her. I had the feeling that if I saw her away from West Lodge I wouldn't even recognise her.

'Well,' I said at last, 'it certainly is very strange.'

Mrs Wilmot seized upon this rather fatuous remark as if I had said something quite original.

'Yes, it *is*, very strange. Quite inexplicable, in fact.'

I suddenly thought of something.

'Her sister, up in Scotland, is very ill. Surely she must have gone up there to see her!'

'Mrs Douglas telephoned them. They've had no word either. Well, there was a letter to her sister a few weeks ago, just a short note, and that's all.'

'Oh.' I felt deflated. 'Have the police put her on their missing persons list? Are they looking for her?'

'Well, of course, in view of her age they have to take it seriously. But, as the Inspector pointed out, she did go off of her own volition, nobody *kidnapped* her or anything. And it isn't as if she's senile. I mean, she's perfectly aware of what she's doing and if, as he said, she chooses to go away, that's her business. It's all very awkward. She could have lost her memory or anything.'

'I suppose people do,' I said doubtfully, 'though I've never actually come across anyone who has.'

'Anyway,' Mrs Wilmot continued, 'after her most recent check-up Dr Hughes said that she was quite *fit*.'

'Thelma seemed to think that her angina was serious,' I said.

'Oh dear me, no. Just a slight murmur, he said. I was surprised that Mrs Douglas made so much of it. A lot of our residents lead quite active lives with much worse heart conditions.'

'If she had been taken ill you or the police would certainly have heard by now. But it really is unlike her to have gone off without telling you.'

'That's what I told the Inspector. Such a *considerate* person Mrs Rossiter always was.'

I noticed that Mrs Wilmot was speaking of her in the past tense.

'I'm sure there must be some perfectly rational explanation of it all,' I said. 'Elderly ladies don't just disappear into thin air!'

'Well, Mrs Rossiter certainly seems to have done so,' Mrs Wilmot said sharply and I realised what a difficult situation it must be for her.

'Have the police seen the taxi driver, Ed Cooper?' I asked. 'I know him quite well, actually. He's a very nice man—he does some driving for the hospital service,'

'Well, I dare say he's perfectly respectable, but it was unfortunate that she couldn't get Mr Simpson; such a reliable man, we always use him when we can. But all this man Cooper could tell them was that he took Mrs Rossiter into Taunton and dropped her off in Church Square. He asked if she wanted him to wait for her, to take her back, but she said that she'd get the bus. She often did that—she said she liked the ride. The bus goes the long way, round through the villages and she used to say she enjoyed seeing places she used to know. I must say I can't stand bus journeys myself, all that stopping and starting. But Mrs Rossiter had some funny little ways.'

There was a tap on the door and Ivy came in.

'Please, Mrs Wilmot, Mr Palgrave has had one of his turns again and Lily thinks you ought to call Dr Randall.'

Mrs Wilmot gave an exclamation of annoyance. 'As if I hadn't got enough to cope with at the moment!'

I got up to go. 'Please do let me know the minute there's any news.'

'Yes, of course.'

She was already at the telephone and spoke absently.

I went along to Mrs Jankiewicz's room, eager to hear what she had to say. But she was in a difficult mood, irritable and disinclined to discuss the matter.

'A great upheaval—everything is disorganised since Tuesday. Police everywhere talking to people, poking and prying into her life. Is her own affair.'

'But something awful may have happened to her.'

'Perhaps—perhaps not.'

She continued to complain about various minor disruptions and I saw that she didn't want to talk. I was used to her moods and I thought that it might be one of the days when she was in a lot of pain. It also occurred to me that she must be upset and missing Mrs Rossiter, who was her only friend at West Lodge, very badly.

'I won't stay now,' I said, 'but I'll pop back tomorrow and see if there's any news.'

Mrs Jankiewicz smiled grimly. 'I will be here,' she said.

Outside in the corridor a sudden thought

crossed my mind and I went up the stairs to Mrs Rossiter's room. I looked up and down the passage but there was no one about. The staff no doubt were all busy with poor Mr Palgrave and his nasty turn. Rather nervously I tried the door, found it was unlocked and slipped into the room, closing it cautiously behind me. The room looked just as it always did; nothing seemed to have been moved. I went over to the desk and pulled open the top drawer. There was no cache of sleeping tablets. I tried all the other drawers but they weren't anywhere. On an impulse I went over to the wardrobe and looked inside. As far as I could tell all her clothes were there.

I heard a movement in the passage outside and froze, but the footsteps passed. Thoroughly unnerved, I opened the door slightly and saw a figure with two walking sticks at the end of the corridor. Feeling like someone in a thriller, I slipped out of the room, down the stairs and into the street, where I stood trembling slightly with mixed feelings of guilt and exhilaration.

I went and leaned on the harbour wall to get my breath back (I felt as if I had been holding it for the last five minutes) and considered what I had found. Or, rather, not found. Had Mrs Rossiter thrown the tablets away? This seemed unlikely in view of the fact that she had kept them so carefully for what must have been several weeks. But if she *had* taken them with her? Then the implications were dreadful.

The tide was out and the small sailing dinghies and larger motor boats leaned sideways in the mud of the harbour. Early holiday-makers sat on benches outside the Pier public house, or sat on the sea wall eating ice-creams. Everything looked so normal—it seemed impossible to think that somewhere Mrs Rossiter was dead. But that's nonsense, I told myself. If she had taken the sleeping tablets, her body would have been found by now. And yet … she could have bought a bottle of whisky in Taunton, taken a bus to one of the villages and walked up through the woods. She knew the area well. Parts of the Quantocks are very remote; a body could remain undiscovered for a long time.

A family group, a young mother, father and small child, passed me, the child scampering in front of his parents who chased him, laughing. Why would she kill herself? She had seemed sad when I saw her last, depressed, perhaps after her flu. It might have been that she saw no point in going on, living at West Lodge, gradually sinking into helplessness and dependency like the other old people there. Whatever affection she might have had for Thelma had been gradually eroded by her daughter's selfishness and indifference; her son was far away, her sister dying. Wouldn't it be better to go while one still had one's faculties, before old age took away the final pleasures that made life bearable? Had Mrs Rossiter made the ultimate choice?

It occurred to me that Mrs Jankiewicz must have made the same deductions. She knew about the sleeping tablets; she knew that Mrs Rossiter had been depressed. Perhaps that was why she had been so moody today, hardly liking to voice such terrible thoughts, even to me. I simply didn't know what to do. If she had already taken the tablets then nothing I could tell anyone would do any good. But suppose she was still making up her mind, sitting in some hotel room, screwing up her courage— what then?

I stood there for a long time, seeing but not seeing the life going on around me. Eventually I left the harbour and walked back along the promenade. All her life Mrs Rossiter had been subject to the will of other people. It seemed only right that she should make this final decision for herself.

CHAPTER FOUR

After a few days of cold and rain I woke up one morning to brilliant sunshine and decided that I could put off no longer the tiresome business of bathing the dogs. Tris, my West Highland terrier, actively dislikes water so I do him first while I still feel quite strong. Tessa, as befits a spaniel, enjoys the water but thinks the whole thing is a delightful game and usually contrives to soak me and everything else within reach. I had just managed to get them both more or less rubbed down when the doorbell rang. The dogs, half dry, broke away and rushed out from the kitchen into the hall, barking excitedly and scattering water-drops as they went. I pushed them to one side and half-opened the door as best I could. Thelma was standing on the doorstep.

I seized the dogs by their scruffs and bundled them back into the kitchen and then came back to find Thelma standing in the hall. One glimpse of my reflection in the hall mirror made me wish I could shut myself in the kitchen with the dogs. I was wearing a dreadful old blouse and skirt that I keep for doing messy jobs. As well as being old and unappealing, they were now heavily splashed with water and dog shampoo. I had no make-up on and my hair was hanging damply (and lankly) round my red and shiny face.

'I'm so sorry,' I said rather breathlessly, 'I was washing the dogs.'

'Oh yes, you always did have animals.'

She made it sound like some awful disease.

I led her into the sitting room and mentally groaned. I had embarked on the dog-washing straight after breakfast, before I had done any tidying up and the room was just as I had left it the night before. Then I had had a sudden fit of rearranging some of my books and there were piles of them on the floor as well as a dirty coffee cup (me), a dog bowl (Tris), an empty saucer (Foss) and a half-chewed Bonio (Tessa).

'Oh dear,' I said helplessly, 'I'm afraid I haven't got around to clearing up this morning. Do, please, sit down.'

She removed a pile of newspaper cuttings from one of the chairs and sat down cautiously.

'Oh, I quite understand. You intellectuals have your minds on higher things.'

I ignored this remark and offered her coffee.

'No, thank you. It's very kind of you but I haven't much time. Goodness ...' She broke off and brought out from the seat of the chair an old cabbage stalk.

'Oh, how awful! It's Tess—she keeps thinking she's a retriever and bringing things in from the compost heap! I do hope it hasn't marked your skirt.' It was just my luck that she was wearing a pale coffee-coloured suit which probably showed every speck.

She cast the cabbage stalk to the ground with some distaste and said impatiently, 'Never mind, I expect it will clean. I wanted to talk to you about Mummy.'

'Oh dear, yes. It must be such a dreadfully worrying time for you. I was absolutely appalled when Mrs Wilmot told me.'

'You really have no idea where she is? I know she used to confide in you and I did hope that you might have a clue as to where she might have gone.'

'I'm sorry. She never gave me any sort of hint that she might be going *anywhere*. And anyway, it really does sound as if she meant to come back—I mean, she told Ivy that she'd be back for tea. I am most horribly afraid that there must have been some sort of accident. I suppose you haven't heard anything else from the police?'

'No, nothing. I don't know what sort of enquiries they've been making but it does seem most peculiar that *no one* seems to have seen her. Can you think of anything at all that might have happened to her?'

'No,' I said. 'Nothing.'

Somehow I couldn't bring myself to tell Thelma about the sleeping tablets. She was Mrs Rossiter's daughter and she did seem very anxious about her mother's disappearance, but I had the feeling that the concern was somehow for herself and not for her mother. It was concern, but not distress.

'It couldn't have happened at a more difficult time,' Thelma said.

'Yes, of course, you've got all these new commitments you were telling me about, those splendid new clients.'

'Yes, there is that—and it really hasn't been easy finding time to come down here and try and sort things out. I blame Mrs Wilmot. What is the use of a matron who lets her old people go wandering about like that, without any sort of check on them?'

'Oh, come now, they're not in prison.'

'Well, you know what I mean. It's quite irresponsible. I shall be writing a very strong letter of complaint to the Managing Director. I suppose I could sue, if something *has* happened to Mummy.'

Her voice became more animated at the prospect and she continued, 'No, all that is inconvenient enough, but what's *really* awkward is that she should be missing now that Aunt Maud is dying.'

'Oh dear, yes. I do see that it must be very upsetting for her. If they've told her, that is. I mean, they may just have kept it from her.'

'What on earth do you mean? Oh, I see. No, it's not that. No, the problem is that if Mummy's still not been found when Aunt Maud dies, it's going to be absolute hell trying to sort out the Trust.'

'The Trust?'

'Yes, my grandfather was a most peculiar old man and he left his money tied up in a really tiresome way.'

'Oh dear. I know that Trusts can be rather odd. Peter used to tell me about some very eccentric ones he had to deal with.'

'Gordon says that all Trusts are set up simply to make money for the lawyers,' she said.

I laughed, though I don't think she meant it as a joke.

'Anyway,' she continued, 'the whole thing is thoroughly ill-conceived. I suppose I'd better tell you, then you'll see how *difficult* all this is going to be for me. I expect you know that my grandfather made a great deal of money in South Africa. He owned three department stores—in Johannesburg and Durban and one in Pietermaritzburg. He sold the Jo'burg and Durban stores in the nineteen-thirties when he brought his daughters back to England—my grandmother had died by then. But he wouldn't sell the Pietermaritzburg store. It was the first one he opened and somehow he felt sentimental about it, I suppose.' Her tone nicely combined respect for her grandfather's business acumen and contempt for his sentiment. 'When Mummy and Aunt Maud married, he set up this Trust. They would each have a moiety—that's a share,' she explained condescendingly. (I didn't remind her that I had been married for over twenty years to a solicitor.) 'A share of the interest on the money he got from the sale of the two stores. It was over a million then, in the 'thirties—and a million *was* a million in those days. And, of course, it was pretty shrewdly invested. He was a good businessman. I suppose,' she said complacently, 'that's where *I* get it from. Anyway, under the Trust Mummy and Aunt Maud inherited the interest, not the capital, and could only bequeath it to their children— not to their husbands. For some reason

Grandfather never had a very high opinion of Daddy's business sense and he always said that Uncle James would never make old bones—and do you know, he was right, because Uncle James died only ten years after they were married.'

'Goodness!' I said, quite overwhelmed by all this financial detail. 'The problems of wealth. But what happens to the capital?'

'Oh, that remains intact in the Trust, rather like an entail, so that the interest continues through the generations. *But*'—and here her lips set in a thin line of disapproval—'there's the question of the third department store.'

'The one in Pietermaritzburg?'

'Yes. He had this thing about keeping it in the family. So he said in his will that it must always remain a private company and it must also be kept intact, under one owner. The company mustn't ever be divided up but must go to the heir—the eldest child, whether male or female—of his surviving daughter.'

'So that if your aunt Maud dies first, then your mother's heir—and that would be you, because you're older than Alan—will inherit it, but if your mother dies *before* your aunt Maud, then your cousin Marion will get it.'

'Exactly. And the amount of money is quite staggering. You see, in addition to the day-to-day profits of the business, and it's a really big concern now, there's all the money from it (and the interest on *that*) that's been mounting up

67

since Grandfather died. That's in another Trust fund. You see what I mean about lawyers; they must have made a fortune out of it already!'

I decided to ignore this slight on the legal profession. 'It does seem a very complicated situation. And, as you say, there is a great deal of money involved.'

'Exactly.' Her voice rose and she became more excited than I had ever seen her. 'You see how monstrous it is—and you can see how unbelievably difficult it is that Mummy should have disappeared just now when Aunt Maud is on her last legs.'

'Yes, I do see…'

'I bet Marion can't wait to get her hands on that money—and that playboy husband of hers, he's never done a day's work in his life; they've just sponged off Aunt Maud all these years. It's so *unfair* when you think how hard Gordon and I have worked and how much difference it would make to the business to have that sort of extra capital just now. I'm sure that if Grandfather were alive he would see that *we* ought to have it.'

I refrained from pointing out that if her grandfather were alive the situation wouldn't have arisen and chose another tack. 'I don't think I've ever met Marion's husband.'

'Van, they call him. He's Dutch. Such a *peculiar* thing to marry a Dutchman! He's supposed to be a painter, but I've never heard

68

that he's sold any of his pictures. They've lived for ages with Aunt Maud in that dreary house just outside Inverness. They've got a pack of unruly children, I can't remember how many. They used to come down and stay with us sometimes—I can't think why. Daddy always made it perfectly clear that they weren't welcome, but you know how thick-skinned some people are. And Mummy's always been rather silly and sentimental about Family, as she calls it.'

A sudden tapping at the window made her turn sharply.

'Oh, don't be alarmed. It's Foss, my cat, he wants to come in.'

I got up and unlatched the window and Foss leapt down with a loud cry. With that particular instinct cats have for annoying people who dislike them, he made straight for Thelma and jumped up on to her lap, where he kneaded her skirt with his claws, thereby finishing its destruction. Thelma, in her turn, uttered a cry that was almost Siamese in its intensity, and I rushed over to remove my errant animal. With some difficulty I managed to unhook his claws and, lifting him off in spite of his very vocal protests, pushed him outside the door, where he continued to make his feelings known.

In some trepidation I turned back to Thelma.

'Oh dear, I'm so sorry. I do hope he hasn't

pulled too many threads. Sometimes you can pull them back from the other side—such an *attractive* skirt...'

It was a measure of her preoccupation with things financial that she didn't make any cutting remarks about uncontrollable animals. Ignoring my incoherent babbling, she said, 'You do realise how absolutely vital it is that we find Mummy immediately. Otherwise the legal complications that will arise when Aunt Maud dies will be appalling—it will cost a fortune! Simon—he's our solicitor—is marvellous, but you know how the money gets simply *eaten up* by any sort of protracted legal wrangle. So are you *sure* there's nothing you can tell me that might throw any light on what can have happened to her?'

I decided then that wild horses wouldn't make me tell Thelma about the sleeping tablets. In fact I was so disgusted by her blatantly mercenary attitude that I could hardly bring myself to be civil.

'No,' I said curtly, 'I've told you. I know nothing.'

My unaccustomed tone seemed to make her suspicious and she gave me a hard stare before she got to her feet and picked up her handbag.

'Well, if you do hear anything, please get in touch. You have my number—just a minute, I'll give you the office one as well.'

She opened her bag and found a business card which she handed to me. I took it without looking at it and went to open the door.

'Have you got your car here?'

'Yes, I drove down. British Rail is quite hopeless nowadays.'

A black BMW was parked in the drive but I didn't go with her as she got into it, nor did I wave as she drove away. I just stood in the doorway until she was out of sight.

Foss was in the kitchen when I went in, sitting hopefully on the draining-board, waiting for someone to turn on the tap so that he could bat at the water. I snatched him up and hugged him, which surprised but did not displease him.

'Oh, Foss,' I said, 'what a *good* boy you are! Destroying Thelma's beastly skirt like that!'

He opened his large blue eyes and regarded me benevolently.

'What an unspeakable person she is! How dear Mrs R. could have produced such a foul daughter...'

I put Foss back on to the draining-board and absently turned on the tap for him. As the water dribbled into the sink I considered the strange financial arrangements that Thelma had told me about. For the first time I contemplated the possibility that Mrs Rossiter's disappearance might have been engineered by someone who wanted her out of the way. That she might have been abducted, even killed. The idea seemed fantastic—such things could not happen in a place like

71

Taviscombe. 'What, in our house!' Lady Macbeth's words echoed through my head in that irritating way that quotations sometimes do, going round and round meaninglessly.

The people who would benefit most from her disappearance would, I supposed, be Marion and her husband. I tried to remember my rare meetings with Marion, when we were all children and she had come down occasionally to stay at the Manor. I had a vague recollection of a tall, rather awkward girl, who always seemed to be plunging about—clumsy, too. I remembered an unpleasant scene with Colonel Rossiter when she had somehow contrived to break a valuable Chinese vase. And she had apparently plunged into relationships in the same awkward way. I recalled confidential grown-up conversations between Mrs Rossiter and my mother, lowered voices which I heard with one ear while I was flicking over the pages of *Country Life* on the blessed occasions when Thelma wasn't there. Maud, it seemed, was very worried about Marion. She had taken up with a rock-and-roll singer, with an actor, with a *plumber* ... The plumber was bought off by Maud, the rest had drifted away. Marion had settled down, and taken a secretarial course, was going to train as a physiotherapist, had gone to Holland as an au pair. She came back from Holland with a Dutch husband. From Maud's point of view, I think it suited her to have Marion and her family living with her. As

Thelma had said, what the Dutchman wanted was to be maintained in a comfortable style so that he could go on painting and Marion seemed to have settled for family life and a lot of children.

But their pleasant life-style would still go on when Maud was dead. Marion would inherit her mother's interest in the capital; they would be no worse off. But people do strange things when a lot of money is involved, and a million pounds *is* a lot of money. If they had arranged to meet Mrs Rossiter in Taunton, had driven her to some lonely spot in the Quantocks ... No. These were silly morbid imaginings—more suited to one of those television thrillers that caused Mrs Jankiewicz so much disquiet. I turned the tap off briskly and went in to tidy up the sitting room.

After my housework I changed into something more respectable and put the now clean and dry dogs into the car to take them down to the beach for a run. I also thought that the sea air might blow away the dismal and unhealthy thoughts that were churning round in my mind.

Although it was a lovely sunny day and the Bristol Channel was looking almost a Mediterranean blue, the holiday season hadn't begun so the beach was pleasantly deserted. I slithered down over the pebbles and let the dogs off their leads. They rushed madly along the sand and back to me and then in wide circles, barking delightedly. I wished that I could plunge so quickly and easily into that same mindless bliss. I walked slowly after them, stooping occasionally to pick up a shell or examine a piece of driftwood, trying to empty my mind of thought.

I was aware of the dogs rushing up to another person also walking a dog and I quickened my steps. It was Ed Cooper, the taxi driver who had taken Mrs Rossiter into Taunton. I went towards him, calling to Tris and Tess.

'Hello, Mr Cooper. How are you? Are my dogs being a nuisance?'

'No, m'dear, my old Bess likes a romp.'

The dogs were all rushing about together in what seemed a friendly fashion, so I turned to Mr Cooper. We made polite conversation about the weather and the Red Cross and then I said, 'What a strange thing that was at West Lodge—Mrs Rossiter going off like that!'

He looked annoyed and muttered something about people trying to put the blame on someone who was only doing his job.

'Not on you, surely! That would be ridiculous!'

My vigorous response seemed to hearten him and he continued more coherently.

'Well, here's the way it is. I reckon no one wants to take the blame for the old lady's disappearance, so they all had a go at me!'

'Had a go?'

'Well, that Mrs Wilmot saying I shouldn't have let her come back on her own. I ask you, 'tisn't for me to say what my ladies should do, they wouldn't like it. And it weren't as if she wasn't all there, if you see what I mean, m'dear—she were quite sharp, a very nice lady, very friendly. I've driven her a couple of times and she always sits in front with me and chats—not like some of them, sitting in the back and never speaking a word, like I were part of the car!'

'What did she chat about when you were driving up to Taunton?'

'Oh, things in general. Quite a bit about my garden. She liked a nice garden, always used to comment on those we passed, what they had in them and such. I think she missed her flowers in that place. What else? Now, let me think. She were asking me about my boy Dave. I'd told her about him last time I drove her—he's got this muscular dystrophy, you know what I mean? And he's had to go into this institution for a bit, just to learn how to go on, then we can have him home again. Anyhow, Mrs Rossiter, she remembered and asked about him, very kindly. As a matter of fact'—he paused and looked at me cautiously 'she gave me a whole tenner as a tip. I didn't want to take it—well, it were too much—but she said it were to buy something to take to the boy when the wife and I went to see him.'

'That was just like her!' I exclaimed.

'I never asked ...' he said defensively.

'I'm sure you didn't. No, she loved children.'

'I didn't tell that Mrs Wilmot about it, either. Or Sergeant Page. They might have thought I were up to something.'

'Oh, you saw the police?'

'Sergeant Page came round to my house. Gave my wife a nasty turn to find him on the doorstep when she got back from shopping, I can tell you. She thought something had happened to me. Anyway, he asked me where I'd dropped Mrs Rossiter in Taunton—it were in Church Square, back of Marks and Spencer. A lot of my ladies like to be dropped there. Handy for the shopping, you see.'

'And that was the last you saw of her?'

He hesitated for a moment and then said, 'Well, there were something. But nothing I could swear to.'

'How do you mean?'

'Well, I didn't mention it to Mrs Wilmot. Her going on at me like that, I weren't going to say no more than I had to. Well, you can understand how I felt, m'dear. And that Sergeant Page—very officious he is, you should have heard the way he went on that time when one of my braking lights were a bit dodgy. I tried to explain how it was, but all he'd say were, "The facts, sir, that's all I want, not excuses." All sarcastic. So, you see, I didn't think it were no use telling him something I only sort of noticed out of the corner of my eye,

76

you might say. Not a *fact*,' he said with heavy irony.

'What did you see?' I asked.

'Well, it were like this, m'dear. I had that tenner from Mrs Rossiter and while I were in Taunton I thought I'd go and get the boy some of those special paints—poster paints they call them—from that art shop round the back of the precinct. Dave, he's very keen on his painting. The pictures don't look like anything you'd recognise, though his mother thinks the world of them, but he likes doing them and they say it does him good. Anyway I puts the car in that car park down by the river and I were just walking through to that machine for my ticket when I thought I saw Mrs Rossiter.'

'You thought?'

'Well, it were just a glimpse, through the parked cars. It looked like she were talking to a man and a woman and then the man took her arm and they all got into a car.'

'What were they like, the man and the woman?'

'Couldn't really say, m'dear. They had their backs to me.'

'Were they old or young?'

'Couldn't properly tell. It were only a quick glimpse, and it had come on to rain a bit by then and they were both wearing macs. He had on a hat, some kind of tweed fishing hat, and she had a scarf tied round her head. You know how it is when you can't see people's faces.'

'Yes, of course. What sort of car?'

'Some sort of Ford, an Escort I think, black—but I could be mistaken. I could be mistaken about the whole thing. I mean, it might not have been Mrs Rossiter at all.'

'How do you mean?'

'Well, this lady were wearing a mac, like Mrs Rossiter were, but she'd got a scarf tied round her head too, and Mrs Rossiter, she hadn't been wearing one of them when I dropped her off. Though, of course, it weren't raining then. But you see how I can't tell anyone, when it's all sort of vague. I don't want them going on at me and coming bothering the wife again. She's got enough to fret about with the boy...'

'Yes, I can see that,' I said doubtfully.

'Any road, I've told you now, m'dear. You see what you make of it.'

He bent to pat his dog, which had left my two investigating a rock pool and returned to her master.

'Good girl, Bess. Well, I must be off, m'dear. The wife'll have the dinner waiting. You won't let on what I told you?'

'No, of course not. I hope your boy is home soon.' He gave me a sort of salute and went off across the sands, his dog at his heels.

I stood in a daze, thinking about what he had told me. Now Mrs Rossiter's disappearance seemed much more sinister. Could she have been kidnapped? Surely not—not in Taunton and in broad daylight! My thoughts returned to Marion and her husband. A man and a woman. She knew them, would naturally trust them, happily get into a car and be driven away—to what? To be murdered? The death of a frail old lady, with a heart condition, could easily be passed off as an accident.

I felt I ought to tell the police, but then Mr Cooper had told me his story in confidence. If I went to the police now he would be in trouble for suppressing evidence, or whatever they called it. Besides, he *might* have been mistaken. But somehow I knew that he was not. In my mind's eye was the picture of Mrs Rossiter, a man's hand on her arm, getting into a car. It was a picture that I knew would stay with me, distressing, haunting even, but I didn't, at the moment, see what I could do about it.

CHAPTER FIVE

I was in the pet shop buying a large bag of cat litter and other necessities when I ran into Ella Lydgate. Ella is a civil servant who took early retirement and is thus able to devote her entire life to animals. Whenever anyone finds a stray dog or cat—or budgerigar or tortoise for that matter—it's always Ella they turn to. As often as not she's up and about at five o'clock in the morning crawling under some garden shed in the pale light of dawn to coax out a terrified half-wild cat. She boasts that she's always managed to find a home for every animal that came to her—though sometimes she has cheated a bit and kept the really impossible cases herself. Her little house somehow contrives to remain neat and tidy although she now has eleven cats and three dogs.

'Hello, Ella,' I said. 'Can I give you a hand back to the house with those?'

'Oh, thank you, Sheila, that would be kind. And while you're there I can show you the new photos of Flora and the kittens.'

Flora was a tiny little grey-and-white cat I had found in the woods with two half-starved kittens. I do most sincerely hope that there is a special hell reserved for those who are cruel to children and animals. The poor little creature had obviously been thrown out of a car when her owners discovered that she was pregnant—I can't imagine the sort of people who could do such a thing. With Ella's help I had housed and fed them and helped to tame the kittens and she had found them a home down in Devon where they could all be together. Like most of Ella's rescue attempts, it had a happy ending.

I held the heavy box of tins of cat food while Ella opened the front door. A great cacophony of barking greeted us and two feline shapes dashed past into the front garden.

'Quiet, Pixie! Quiet, Jetty! I'll just go into the kitchen and let them know I'm back. You go into the sitting room. I won't be a minute.'

In the tiny sitting room there were cats on every chair and several on the broad window sill, some with the net curtains caught up over their heads where they were looking out. There were food dishes (mostly licked clean) each on its own plastic mat, cat-litter trays on folded newspapers in two corners of the room and a variety of cat-nip mice, small rubber balls and doggy-chews, but the general effect was one of order. I reflected that my house, with two dogs and one fastidious Siamese, always looked much more chaotic. I wondered enviously how Ella managed it. I picked up a large marmalade cat from the sofa and sat down with it on my lap where it settled comfortably, purring loudly as I stroked it.

Ella came in with one of the numerous albums full of photographs sent to her by the new and loving owners of her protégées. She flipped over the pages and said, 'There! Look how the kittens have grown. They're quite tame now, even that very nervous little grey one.'

As she sat down on the sofa beside me the marmalade cat jumped down and went over to sit on Ella's lap instead—animals always preferred Ella to anyone else.

'Now then, Sandy!' she reproved him. 'What will Sheila think of your manners, abandoning her like that!'

'He's beautiful,' I said, 'such a lovely coat.'

I suddenly thought of something.

'Did you call him Sandy? Was he Mrs Rossiter's cat? I thought I recognised him.'

'That's right. Poor soul, she was dreadfully upset about not being able to keep him when she went into West Lodge. She loved that cat, didn't she, Sandy?' The cat looked up at her and she bent and put her face against his head. 'Her daughter, what's her name, Thelma, she wanted her mother to have him put down. Can you imagine? Well, Mrs Rossiter wouldn't do it. She came to me in such a state! Her daughter had made all the arrangements about West Lodge and poor Mrs Rossiter didn't feel she could go against her. Well, you know what a meek little person she is; the soul of kindness, could never say boo to a goose. There was Thelma saying that Sandy had had a good life—he's fifteen—and that it would be the kindest thing to have him put to sleep and that her mother had to go into West Lodge because she couldn't manage on her own any more.'

'How awful!'

'Well, we couldn't let a beautiful boy like this be put to sleep, could we? So I said I'd take him. Mrs Rossiter knew he'd be all right with me.'

'Bless you, Ella. What would we all do without you!'

'Well, one more doesn't make much difference and it's not easy finding a home for an elderly gentleman of fifteen. Though I must say,' she continued, 'it never seemed to me right to say that Mrs Rossiter couldn't look after herself. Not in that big house, maybe, but she could have had a nice little flat, a ground floor one with a bit of garden for Sandy. But that daughter of hers always did rule the roost and I don't suppose she wanted to have to bother about her mother, finding a flat and so forth. Easier to put her into a home and have poor Sandy here put down. Honestly, Sheila, sometimes I'm really glad I've got no family, only the animals. *They* never let you down!'

'I know. I mean, I'm lucky that Michael is so marvellous—when I think of Thelma!—but there have been times, when Mother and Peter died and Michael was away in Oxford, when I don't think I could have got through if it hadn't been for the animals.'

We looked at each other and smiled.

'Idiots, aren't we?' I said. 'Still, I'd rather be silly about animals than be like the Thelmas of this world. But, oh dear, poor Mrs Rossiter!'

'She comes round sometimes to see him. She sits here on this sofa with him on her lap and has a little weep and I make us a cup of tea and I think she goes away feeling better.'

'I'm sure she does.'

'She was round here last week.'

'What!'

'Last Monday, was it? Yes, that's right, because that was the day I had to take Pixie to Mr Hawkins to have her booster shot and she was waiting on the doorstep when I got back.'

'How did she seem?'

'Funny you should ask that,' Ella said. 'She seemed a bit agitated, a bit emotional, if you know what I mean. She didn't stay long, but when she hugged Sandy here it seemed as if she couldn't bear to let him go. It was worse, almost, than when she brought him. And a funny thing—she made me take some money for his keep. I didn't want to—well, you know how I feel; as long as I can manage on my little pension—but she was so insistent that in the end I took it, but it didn't feel right...'

'I honestly don't know how you manage,' I said, 'what with the price of cat food, not to mention Kittylitta. But did she say anything? Mrs Rossiter, I mean.'

'Nothing special, it was just her manner, really. Why?'

I told Ella about Mrs Rossiter's disappearance.

'Well,' she said, 'it's almost as if she knew she wouldn't be coming back. Coming to see Sandy and going away so upset like that.'

'It does seem strange. But she couldn't have gone off somewhere deliberately without telling anyone where she was going. You know what she was like; she wouldn't have made people upset like that for the world. Besides, where could she have gone? She only had Thelma and her sister in Scotland, and we know she's not with either of them.'

We sat silently for a moment and then Ella

said, 'Well, whatever's happened to her, poor soul, at least she knows that Sandy's well cared for.'

She got to her feet and put the marmalade cat back on to my lap.

'I'll go and put the kettle on,' she said.

I sat absently stroking his fine head and considered what Ella had told me. If Mrs Rossiter had gone off somewhere to take her own life, most probably she would have gone to say goodbye to Sandy and she would certainly have been very emotional. If, on the other hand, she'd gone to meet someone in Taunton, as Mr Cooper's story seemed to imply, then perhaps she had expected to be away for some time. But in that case, why had she acted so out of character and said she'd be back for tea when she must have known that she wouldn't?

The problem seemed insoluble. I looked round the room at the cats. Each was sitting in what was obviously its 'own' place. Some were dozing, some were regarding me with interest and curiosity, some were occupied with their own mysterious feline thoughts, but all looked perfectly content, accepting their lot with equanimity. I thought how much better adjusted they were than their human counterparts, also in their last refuge, at West Lodge. But then what they had here was not just food and shelter and impersonal care, but Ella's love, and that, of course, made all the difference.

After I left Ella's I went into Stevens's to buy a bottle of fertiliser for my tomato plants. Stevens's is the last really old-fashioned shop we have in Taviscombe. It is basically a proper ironmonger's where men in brown overalls will still sell you half a dozen screws, that is, if you are prepared to wait upwards of half an hour while they engage other (male) customers in mysterious conversations which abound in phrases like 'medium-sized mole' and 'laminated five-by-two'. In addition they have a gardening section, where proper tools like bill-hooks and scythe-heads are all jumbled up with modern gadgets for trouble-free gardening and great sacks full of broad beans, peas and runner-bean seed. Round the corner are shelves of kitchenware and plastic cups and plates for picnics, as well as the boxed sets of glasses, plated toast racks and gift packs of ovenware which usually feature prominently among the presents at a Taviscombe wedding.

I was threading my way cautiously around this section of the shop (the display shelves were piled so high that one was in constant danger of bringing the whole thing crashing to the ground) when I found myself face to face with Ivy.

'Oh, Mrs Malory! Fancy bumping into you. I was going to come and see you tomorrow.'

'Ivy, how nice. Was it something special? Though, of course, you know I'm always glad to see you.'

'It's for a reference.'

'A reference? But—what for—I mean, I thought you were quite settled at West Lodge. I'm sure Mrs Wilmot would be very sorry to see you go.'

Ivy made a sound halfway between a snort and a sob.

'Well, she wasn't—she's given me the sack!'

'No! She couldn't!'

'Well, as good as—and it's so *unfair*, Mrs Malory!'

Her voice rose and there were tears in her eyes. Other customers turned their heads to look at us curiously.

'Look, Ivy,' I said hastily, 'why don't we pop into the Buttery, it's just across the road. And you can tell me all about it over a nice cup of tea.'

When we were settled at a quiet table with our tea and a slice of orange cake for Ivy ('I shouldn't really, I don't want to spoil my tea—but it does look so tempting') she was a little calmer.

'Now then, Ivy, tell me all about it. Whatever happened?'

'Well, it was when Mrs Rossiter went off like that. You can imagine what a stew everything was in, with the police there and Mrs Rossiter's daughter laying down the law—you know the way she does—and Mrs Wilmot in such a state. Talk about bad-tempered. I said to Maureen (she helps Cook in the kitchen), Maureen, I said, you'd think it was *our* fault Mrs Rossiter's gone off the way her ladyship goes on at us. We can't seem to do anything right.'

Ivy cut her cake into a number of minute pieces and conveyed one of them neatly to her mouth.

I said soothingly, 'I expect she's been very worried, but it does seem hard that she should take it out on you.'

'That's right. Anyway. It was on the Tuesday that Mrs Rossiter went and what with one thing and another I didn't get to give her room a good clean until the Thursday. Well, the police said we shouldn't touch anything and they went through all her things—looking for clues, I suppose, though I don't think they had any call to look through the poor lady's diary. Not that they found anything, just appointments with the dentist and people's birthdays. I don't suppose the poor thing had much else to put in her diary anyway, in that miserable place! Where was I? Oh yes, well, I gave the room a good hoovering and I was just going to dust round when her ladyship came in. You know how she is, she always has to stand there and watch you working, just to see if she can find fault. Well, as I say, I was standing there with the duster in my hand when she suddenly said, "What's become of Mrs Rossiter's ivory figurine?" I expect you know the piece she meant, Mrs Malory; it's that little statue of a deer. She used to keep it on the top of her desk with some photographs.'

'Yes, I know the one you mean.'

'I said, "I don't know, I'm sure. Perhaps it's slipped down behind the desk." So we pulled the desk out but it wasn't there. Then she flew into quite a rage and as good as accused me of stealing it. "What will Mrs Douglas think!" she kept saying. Though it seems to me, Mrs Malory, if your poor mother's gone missing like that you really won't be bothered if an ornament's been mislaid!'

I thought that Thelma's reaction would depend on the value of the figurine. '"The police will have to be told immediately," she said, and I said, "Well, perhaps *they've* taken it, because they were the last people in Mrs Rossiter's room, not me." Then she really flared up and said that if I was going to be impertinent I would really have to go. Well, you know me, Mrs Malory, that's not me at all. I didn't mean the police had stolen it—I thought it might have been evidence or something. Oh, I *was* upset! So I said that I was certainly not going to stay in a place where I was accused of stealing and I walked right out. You'd have done the same, Mrs Malory. And I haven't been back. Maureen put my bits and bobs together—my overalls and my old shoes that I keep there—and brought them round for me the next day. And I won't go back, Mrs Malory, not if she was to go down on her knees. Anyway I've got this job at Brockwell Lodge—it's a lovely place, used to be a gentleman's residence—and not so many patients either. Captain and Mrs Fairweather (he used to be in the Navy) run it and they're ever so nice. Well, they know how things should be done, they were brought up to it, like your dear mother. They were ever so pleased to have me but, of course, I wasn't going to ask Mrs Wilmot for a reference, which is why I was coming to see you to ask you to speak for me.'

'Yes, of course, Ivy, I should be delighted. I think the Fairweathers are very lucky to have got you.'

Privately, I feared that Brockwell Lodge would probably last no longer than many similar residential homes for the elderly which had mushroomed in Taviscombe in the last five or six years. They tended to be run by ex-Service people, some, like the Fairweathers, full of good intentions, genuinely wanting to give value for money but often hopeless at managing the business side of things, gradually losing their capital and finally selling out at a loss. There were others run strictly for profit by the more unscrupulous, who provided only the minimum that would get them by the Ministry Inspectors; grim places where unsympathetic relatives left their now burdensome parents to wait for death. There were quite a few of these. However, I didn't feel that this was the time to voice my feelings about Brockwell Lodge to

Ivy.

'I'll write a reference tonight so that you can take it to Captain Fairweather tomorrow.'

'Oh, thank you, Mrs Malory. They know I was at West Lodge, but I didn't tell them exactly why I left. I just said that I didn't get on with Mrs Wilmot. Well, that's true enough, isn't it?'

'That's all right, Ivy, I'll skirt round that point. It's funny, though, about that little figurine. No,' I said hastily as she seemed about to interrupt me, 'no, of course I don't think *you* took it. But I wonder what could have happened to it. Was anyone else in her room—apart from the police, I mean—anyone you didn't know?'

She took a sip of tea and, finding it rather hot, blew delicately into her cup. She put the cup down carefully in the saucer and said, 'Not after she went, no.'

'What do you mean?'

'Well, there was that man—I've only just remembered him, this very minute—with you asking that...'

'What man?'

'It was about ten days before poor Mrs Rossiter went off. In the afternoon, just after dinner—they have it at twelve, you know, so it's over quick and her ladyship can have hers at one on the dot. Anyway, I'd just given Maureen a hand with the clearing up—not that it was my job, but they were short-handed—

and I went to that big cupboard in the kitchen to put some things away and I saw the packets of light-bulbs they keep there, and so *then* I remembered that her ladyship had told me to put a new bulb in the passage, just by the stairs, you know. It's very dark in that corner, quite dangerous for the old people. So I was just going along to do it when I saw this man and he asked me if I could tell him the way to Mrs Rossiter's room.'

'What was he like? Young or old?'

'Well, that I couldn't say, Mrs Malory. Like I said, that corner's very dark and he had his back to the light from the front door, where he'd come in.'

'What did his voice sound like?'

'He was a foreigner, that I can tell you. He had a very funny accent, quite strong it was.'

'What *sort* of accent?'

'Oh, I don't know that! All sound alike to me, foreigners do!'

'Did he find Mrs Rossiter's room?'

'Oh, yes. Well, I told him which way to go and later on, when I was passing her room, I heard voices.'

'I wonder who he was?'

'That I couldn't say, though I wondered at the time if he wasn't something to do with one of those overseas missions. Well, Mrs Rossiter always went to church regular, twice a day some Sundays.' She took another sip of her tea and said reflectively, 'I thought he might be a missionary.'

'Whatever makes you think that?'

'Well, when I was passing the door I thought I heard Mrs Rossiter saying something about Christian duty. Not that I was eavesdropping, mind, that's not me, Mrs Malory, as you know, but she was talking about Christian duty and the foreigner said it was the last chance to save something or someone, I couldn't rightly say which. I suppose it was these poor famine victims that you see on the television, it breaks your heart to see them, poor little mites. And Mrs Rossiter was very generous. I expect he'd come to ask her for money for the mission.'

'I suppose it might have been ... And that's all you heard?'

'Oh yes, like I said, I was just passing the door—I was going to get that end room ready for a new lady—you know poor Mr Robson passed on? A merciful release, you might say, but his poor daughter was ever so upset. Such a nice woman, she was always very pleasant to me.'

'Ivy, I do think you ought to tell Mrs Wilmot about this man.'

Her lips set in a firm line.

'Oh no, Mrs Malory, I couldn't do that. I shan't cross *that* threshold again.' She looked at me triumphantly, pleased with her dramatic statement.

'Well, the police, then.'

'Oh, I couldn't go to the police! They'd ask

me why I wasn't still working there. *They* might think I'd stolen that little statue. No, Mrs Malory, I'll let well alone, thank you very much.'

She picked up a few remaining crumbs of cake on her plate delicately with her finger and put them in her mouth.

'Well, I did enjoy that. I'd better be on my way or Benjy will think I've deserted him.'

Benjy was her budgerigar. I enquired after his health and she said, 'Oh, he's lovely, Mrs Malory, such company. I don't know what I'd do without him!'

Ivy had been a widow for many years, much longer than me, and I reflected that the replacement of a loved one with an animal (or a bird) seemed a very Anglo-Saxon solution; somehow I couldn't see the French or the Italians doing such a thing.

When we parted I made my way slowly down the Avenue to where I had parked my car, wondering what, if anything, Ivy had heard. A foreigner—a man with an accent—talking to Mrs Rossiter about religion ... I really couldn't make head or tail of it. He *could* be from a foreign mission, though somehow that didn't seem quite right. I was still feeling rather dazed from the continuous flow of Ivy's conversation and my mind was even woollier than usual. Actually, I'm never at my best in the late afternoon. I usually pick up about suppertime, after a small glass of something.

Perhaps later on I would be able to make sense of the information that had come my way.

My key was in the car door when I remembered that I hadn't bought my tomato fertiliser after all. With a sigh, I turned round and made my way back up the Avenue.

CHAPTER SIX

That evening I was sitting looking mindlessly at a programme about Impressionist painters on the television. Tessa was sitting heavily on my feet and Foss and Tris were edging me gradually off the sofa as they jockeyed for the best position. I gave a sudden exclamation which made Foss jump down hurriedly from the sofa and then turn to look at me reproachfully.

I looked again at the screen, where a large close-up of Van Gogh's 'Cornfield at Arles' caused me to say aloud, 'Of course—Dutch! Marion's husband!'

Certainly Van, or whatever he was called, was the only foreigner I could think of in connection with Mrs Rossiter. And certainly he—or Marion—had a very strong motive for wanting Mrs Rossiter out of the way before Marion's mother died. He could perfectly well have come down from Scotland to see her. No one knew him in Taviscombe except Thelma, and she wasn't likely to be there. He could quite safely call, pretending that he just happened to be in the area and wanted to give her news of her sister.

Foss jumped back on to my knee and began to knead my skirt with his claws. I always wear an old tweed skirt when I'm on my own in the evenings and so many threads have been pulled that the front has taken on the quality of fine mohair. I stroked Foss's soft dark head and continued to work out my theory, if such it could be called. While he was there, Van could have arranged to meet her in Taunton—for lunch, perhaps—so that she would genuinely have thought that she'd be back for tea. Then, when they met, he could say that he'd just heard from Marion that Maud was much worse, dying, in fact, and was asking for her sister. He'd have a car ready and would say they needed to leave at once and he'd telephone West Lodge when they stopped on the motorway. That would have been the scene that Ed Cooper saw in the car park in Taunton.

I wasn't sure who the woman could have been. Not Marion; presumably she would have been at her mother's bedside. Perhaps one of their daughters? They must be quite grown up by now. Then events could have followed the grim scenario I had considered before. A lonely spot in the Quantocks, somewhere Mrs Rossiter could have got to herself by bus or taxi, and then (my mind shied away from this) they disposed of her so that it would look like an accident when she was discovered. All they had to do was to make sure that the body would be found before Maud died and they would inherit the larger part of old Mr Westlock's immense fortune.

The picture on the television now was the haunting self-portrait of Van Gogh, his head bandaged and his eyes enormous with defeat and despair. It seemed too painful to contemplate so I pressed the remote control and banished the image from the screen, but I couldn't so easily banish the pictures I had conjured up in my mind of Mrs Rossiter in danger and in fear.

On a sudden impulse I stood up and got out my address book. Marion was on my Christmas card list, so I knew where she lived. I got her number from Directory Enquiries and, not knowing in the least what I was going to say, I dialled. The voice that answered was low, pleasant and definitely foreign.

'I do hope I'm not calling at an inconvenient time,' I said, 'but do you think I might have a few words with Marion? She does know me, though we haven't seen each other for years. My name is Sheila Malory.'

'Oh yes, I know, Shei-la.' He gave my name two distinct syllables. 'Marion has spoken of you. When you were children in Taviscombe.' He pronounced it 'Taviscom'. 'I am sure she would be delighted to speak with you. Poor

Marion, everything is very sad for her, for us all, you know. She will be happy to hear a new voice. It will cheer her. Wait one moment and I will fetch her.'

After a few minutes, when I began to wonder what on earth had possessed me to embark on this ridiculous enterprise, Marion picked up the receiver and said, 'Sheila! What a nice surprise! How good of you to call.'

'I just wondered how things were,' I said rather feebly. 'How is your mother?'

'About the same. We've brought her home now. There's nothing more they can do for her in hospital and we thought she'd rather be here than in a hospice. I know they're marvellous but, well, she just wants to lie in her own bed by the window and look out over the loch.'

'Of course. But it must be a dreadful strain for you.'

'Well, it's sad, of course, but she's a marvellous patient and quite cheerful. One good thing, its quite easy to get domestic help up here—our Mrs Buchan is a real treasure—so we can just concentrate on being with her, me, Van and the children. It's been a surprisingly happy time; isn't that strange!' I found it difficult to reconcile this calm, resolute, cheerful woman with the awkward girl I had known, plunging about physically and emotionally. It would seem that Marion had, quite simply, grown up.

'How long has she been back with you?'

98

'Oh, about six weeks now. I'm afraid it can't last much longer, though. The doctor's not very hopeful; he says probably only a few more weeks. She's very frail now.'

'I'm so sorry ... You must be worn out.'

'Yes, well, it's a bit tiring. We've none of us been out of the house, except for the odd hour in Inverness to do the shopping, since she's been back, and that gets a bit wearing. Mrs Buchan would take over, I know, but we feel that time is so precious that we don't really want to be anywhere else. Well, you'll know what it's like. Aunt Edith told me about your mother—I'm sorry, I meant to write, but...'

'Yes, of course. You're lucky to have Van...'

'He's wonderful. Mother adores him, he hardly ever leaves her side. He's taken his easel and painting things into her room now and they sit together and he paints the loch.'

'I'm so glad.'

There was a small pause then Marion said, 'Is there any news of Aunt Edith? Is she all right? Thelma rang in a bit of a state.'

'No, I'm afraid we still don't know what's happened—where she is.'

'It's a most extraordinary thing. Poor little soul, I do hope that nothing awful's happened to her. She was always very kind to me. I used to hate going down there to stay—well, you remember how ghastly that house was. Uncle Julian and Thelma—terrible! Poor Aunt

Edith, they led her a dreadful life, but she always tried to smooth things over when I did something stupid or clumsy (which was quite a lot of the time!). And when we were alone she gave me little treats—chocolates and once a pretty lace collar for a dress, bless her! I do hope she's all right. We haven't told Mother. They weren't very close after they came back to England, but it would worry and upset her. Well, you can imagine.'

'Yes, of course. I'll let you know if there's any news, but it does seem a complete mystery.'

'I bet Thelma's raising hell.'

'You could put it like that.'

'Going on about that bloody Trust, I suppose. That woman is obsessed with money; I suppose she hasn't got anything else.'

'No children, you mean?'

'No children and a husband who is equally obsessed. Anyway, I imagine she didn't want any children. She doesn't like them. She was always foul to my lot whenever we called in to see Aunt Edith when we were in the south.'

'It's probably just as well,' I observed. 'She'd have been a ghastly mother. Just think of it!'

'Don't. No, really Sheila, what can she get out of life? I don't understand it, I mean what's it all for? When she's built up that business, made yet another fortune, what then? Money won't buy you happiness, don't they say? Well, I suppose it's easy enough for me to say that; we've always been comfortable. But it isn't the

100

things that money has bought that I value. Does that sound priggish? I suppose, just now, seeing Mother and what really gives her happiness in these last days, well...'

'You're right, Marion,' I said warmly. 'And it's only at times like this that one actually stops to think things out clearly and set out one's real values.'

'How strange—that's more or less what Van said the other day. I'm glad it's been like this for me and I do, honestly, pity Thelma if all she can think of when her mother is missing is the money. It must be terrible to live without love.'

We talked a little more and then I said, 'I mustn't keep you—you will have things to do.'

'Yes, I must go and settle Mother for the night. Thank you so much for calling, Sheila. I do appreciate it. I'm so happy to have had this talk. Bless you.'

I rang off, feeling thoroughly ashamed of myself.

Of course, it *might* have been a tremendous act, setting an alibi for them all, but somehow I knew it wasn't like that. I remembered clearly enough, from my own experience, the feeling of isolation and self-containment in a household where one of the members is dying. The world outside doesn't seem to exist and one has to make a positive effort to communicate with anyone beyond that circle. I recognised in Marion's voice the same note that must have been in mine in the weeks

101

before Peter died. I was still amazed at the new Marion, so unlike the heedless girl I knew, but she had always been a good-hearted person and such an experience might well have brought out the best in her. And, ultimately, you can always tell, especially over the telephone when there is nothing else to distract you, when someone is really sincere and Marion, I was absolutely positive, was sincere when she said she didn't care about the money.

*   *   *

Next morning I had to nerve myself to go and visit Rosemary's mother in West Lodge. Although she had made a good recovery from her stroke and was certainly marvellously well looked after by Rosemary and the faithful Elsie, Mrs Dudley was bored and had wanted a change of scene. 'And, of course,' Rosemary had said, 'her friend Mrs Bascombe has just gone into West Lodge for a few weeks while her daughter's away, so Mother had to go too. I wouldn't *mind*,' she added, 'if it meant that I could have a little break and it's quite convenient to have her there, under cover, just now, but I have to go down twice a day in case she wants anything special—and to prove to Mrs Wilmot and all the other patients what a devoted daughter she has!' So I said I'd pop in one morning—not because I wanted to see Mrs Dudley, but because I thought it might ease things a little for Rosemary.

Armed with a pot of primulas I made my way to West Lodge.

Mrs Dudley, expensively dressed, her face carefully made up and her hair recently set, was sitting in an armchair in one of the best rooms, looking out over the promenade and the sea. I saw that she had already settled in. There were vases of flowers, a box of chocolate mints, several of the more expensive magazines and a new biography of a minor member of the royal family.

She greeted me with a gracious smile and looked critically at the primulas.

'How kind of you, my dear. I must make sure they water them properly; primulas do tend to die off in a warm atmosphere.'

'You look very comfortable,' I said, hoping to placate her.

'They do their best, I suppose, and certainly they charge enough, but the service isn't what I'm used to. Just press that bell, my dear, for coffee.'

'Anyway, you've got a nice view.'

She cast a disparaging look at the promenade below. 'I must say, it doesn't give me any pleasure to see how dreadfully Taviscombe has gone down these days. Just look at those terrible people!'

A family party, a mother, father and two small children, all wearing brightly coloured Bermuda shorts and T-shirts, were making their way down the steps to the beach. A little further along a young couple were unloading a windsurfing board from the roof of their car, watched with interest by two elderly ladies with white cardigans over their summer dresses.

'Well,' I said rather feebly, 'it is holiday time.'

'In the old days,' Mrs Dudley, said, 'we never used to have summer visitors like *that*. People used to come down for the hunting—and, before the war, they used to play polo on the Castle lawns. We had members of the aristocracy and Maharajahs. Indian princes, you know,' she explained, in case I did not fully appreciate past grandeur. 'They hired houses, of course. Polo is still played in the best circles, but you couldn't expect Prince Charles to come down here, not with the sort of riff-raff we get in the town nowadays.'

Maureen from the kitchen, now apparently promoted to Ivy's job, put her head round the door.

'Did you ring, then?' she enquired.

Mrs Dudley stiffened. 'Please come into the room properly; I cannot talk to anyone half in and half out of a doorway. That's better. Now we would like some coffee. In a proper pot and on a tray. And some decent biscuits. The last lot you brought me were dry and one of them was broken.'

Maureen gave me the ghost of a wink, said, 'Righty-oh,' and left.

'This place is getting very slack,' Mrs Dudley continued. 'But bad as it is, it is still the only nursing home in Taviscombe that I would consider.'

'How are you, now?' I asked. 'I must say you're looking very well.'

'I always make the best of things,' Mrs Dudley said complacently. 'Dr Hughes felt I should have a little extra care and attention. And, of course, I didn't want to be a burden to Rosemary. She leads such a busy life, always running about, doing things for Jilly. I scarcely ever see her these days.'

Her shameless effrontery made me catch my breath and she continued, 'No, in spite of everything, Dr Hughes agreed that West Lodge was the best place for me for a week or so. I did have my doubts, as you can imagine, after that affair with Mrs Rossiter.'

'It still seems to be a complete mystery,' I said. 'We're all very worried.'

'She was always a poor little creature,' Mrs Dudley said. 'I wouldn't be at all surprised if she had lost her memory and was wandering about somewhere. Probably senile.'

'Oh, surely not!' I exclaimed.

Mrs Dudley ignored my interruption as she ignored any contradiction of her opinions.

'A sad little person. I mean, she had that beautiful house and all that money, and what did she make of herself, I ask you! She could have run the county!'

'I don't think she wanted...'

'That's not the point. People like that have a duty. Noblesse oblige. Though, of course, I imagine that was the whole point. Not noblesse at all. She wasn't born to it and that makes all the difference.'

'I don't really think ...' I began but Mrs Dudley swept on.

'Nouveau riche. Her husband, now, Colonel Rossiter, *his* was a very old family—North Devon, related to the Trahernes, the cadet branch, but still ... But old Mr Westlock, well, he was only a tradesman, in quite a small way of business. My mother used to tell me that she remembered him keeping a little drapery shop in East Street in Taunton. That was before the Great War, of course. So many things changed then ...'

'But he made an immense fortune in South Africa,' I said.

'Yes, but it was still trade, whatever you might say—'

She broke off as Maureen came into the room with a tray.

'Sorry, Mrs Wilmot's got the only coffee pot for her elevenses,' she said cheerfully as she slammed the tray down on a small table. 'Still, it's only instant any road, so I don't suppose it'd have tasted any different.'

She was out of the room before Mrs Dudley had time to protest. I handed her a cup of coffee and passed her the plate of biscuits.

'These dreadful thick cups—and plain digestive biscuits—I really will have to have a word with Mrs Wilmot!'

'Did you know Mrs Rossiter before she was married?' I asked to divert her attention from these enormities.

'Oh, yes, indeed. When their father brought them back to England in the late 'twenties, Maud, Edith and I used to meet at dances. Quite plain girls, I always thought, though of course expensively dressed. The county didn't take to them. Mr Westlock had bought a large estate this side of Dulverton. He tried to set himself up as a country gentleman, hunting and shooting and using a stretch of the Barle for fishing, but he was never accepted, not by anyone who mattered. He wanted to get those girls off—especially difficult with the mother dead, though I believe she was quite common, so it might have been a blessing that she died before they came back to England. Of course some of our old families were really quite poor after the war and weren't too choosy about marrying into money, however it had been made. Maud married the son of a baronet but it was a Scottish title and he was the younger son and, anyway, he was very sickly—tuberculosis, I believe—and he died quite young. Maud could have done better for herself, I would have thought, but she seemed to be fond of him.' Mrs Dudley looked faintly surprised, as if she couldn't imagine anyone being fond of a younger son.

'And what about Edith? Wasn't there anyone she was fond of?' I couldn't believe that anyone could have been fond of Colonel Rossiter.

Mrs Dudley seemed pleased by my interest. This was the sort of conversation she liked best of all, picking over the past (discreditable, if possible) of what she called 'our better families'—a combination of snobbery and malice that she greatly enjoyed.

'Edith? No, I don't think so. She was always very subdued, a meek little mouse of a thing, no go in her. Men don't like that, you know. I did hear that she had formed some unsuitable attachment in South Africa, but whatever else he might have been, Mr Westlock was a good father to those girls and saw that they married eligible men.'

'Poor Mrs Rossiter—what was wrong with the young man in South Africa?'

'Oh, I don't know. No money, no family—though that was hardly surprising in a place like South Africa, a dreadfully common country I always think. Worse than Australia, even. No, Julian Rossiter was a difficult man, I do admit that, but he had that splendid house and a position in the county. Considering everything, I think Edith did very well for herself.'

I thought of Colonel Rossiter, standing scowling in the ornate doorway of that large gloomy house, and I shuddered.

'Not that it did old Mr Westlock any good. He died quite soon after Edith married Julian Rossiter—a shooting accident, if you please. The most expensive guns, I believe, but of course, he simply wasn't used to such things.'

She spoke disparagingly, as if only the landed gentry had any right to kill themselves with guns by Holland and Holland or Purdy.

'How sad.'

Poor little Mrs Rossiter, married off against her will to a disagreeable man, her father dead and her sister far away in Scotland. No wonder she had always seemed a sad figure, even to a child. And then to have a daughter like Thelma!

'It was a pity that she had to come into West Lodge,' I said. 'I know that the Manor was too big for her after Colonel Rossiter died, but I would have thought that she could have had a little cottage somewhere, or a flat...'

'Certainly *I* wouldn't have left the Manor,' Mrs Dudley said. 'I always think that people should stay in their own homes as long as they can. I,' she said firmly, 'would never dream of leaving Ashgrove and all my beautiful things. These sort of places are all very well in their way'—her gaze rested contemptuously on the tray with the coffee cups—'but one is used to a certain standard.'

'Well, of course,' I said, 'you do have Elsie to look after you and Rosemary is marvellous.'

'Well, naturally, Elsie is devoted to me. She's been with me for years. She came to me straight from school when she was fourteen,' Mrs Dudley said, blandly ignoring all reference to her daughter, 'so I've been able to train her in my little ways. And, of course, she knows that I've remembered her in my will—something quite substantial.'

I reflected that however substantial Elsie's legacy was she would certainly have earned it.

'Of course,' I pursued, 'you're very lucky that, although Martin's in Doncaster, Rosemary lives down here. Poor Mrs Rossiter—Thelma and Alan are so far away. Though I'm jolly sure that, even if she'd been here, Thelma wouldn't have looked after her mother as Rosemary looks after you!'

'We have always been an exceptionally close and devoted family,' Mrs Dudley said with a degree of self-deception that took my breath away. 'I have always done my very best for my children—left on my own to bring them up from quite an early age—and I know that they feel it is a privilege to do the odd little thing to help their old mother.'

She gave me a smile of saccharine sweetness to which I did not respond and she continued, 'Thelma, of course, is a very good businesswoman. She has a real head on her shoulders. *She* should have been the son. Alan was always a poor thing, took after his mother. All this Africa nonsense, I've no patience with

110

it! No, Thelma realised that her mother couldn't cope on her own and that West Lodge was the only answer.'

'But she could have had a little flat,' I persisted, 'and Annie Fisher would have been perfectly happy to look after her...'

'That woman!' Mrs Dudley cut in sharply. 'Thelma wouldn't have stood for that. She told me several times that she was very worried that Annie Fisher was getting a hold over her mother.'

'What sort of hold? She always seemed a perfectly respectable woman to me, and devoted to Mrs Rossiter.'

'It was some sort of religious sect—I can't remember what they were called. She joined them a little while ago. Thelma was very concerned that she might try to get Mrs Rossiter to make over a lot of money to them. You know what these people are like, they're very persuasive. No, that wouldn't have done at all. I mean, even when she was in West Lodge, I believe Annie Fisher was always in and out to see her.'

'Yes, that's true.'

I wondered why I hadn't heard about Annie's religious conversion, but reflected that as I had always disliked the woman I'd tried to avoid her whenever possible, and Mrs Rossiter and I had other things to talk about.

'So Thelma thought it was the lesser of the two evils that her mother should come here. I mean, it is dreadfully expensive—though, goodness knows, Mrs Rossiter could afford it. And Thelma very sensibly advised her mother to take shares in West Lodge, so naturally the fees were adjusted accordingly.'

No wonder Mrs Wilmot had panicked. She had mislaid not only a patient but a shareholder as well!

'It is no bad thing, really, that the fees should be so high. It does keep out a certain class of people.'

The room was very hot, and suddenly I felt I couldn't bear any more of Mrs Dudley. I gathered up my handbag and gloves and stood up.

'It's been lovely to see you and I'm delighted that you're so much better, but I must be getting on. I must call in and see Mrs Jankiewicz while I'm here.'

Mrs Dudley pursed her lips in disapproval. 'I can't say I approve of letting foreigners in.'

'Oh, come now,' I said sweetly. 'Her cousin is a countess, you know, and the Polish aristocracy is more ancient than ours.'

She looked at me suspiciously, as if uncertain of my seriousness. 'That's as may be—and, as I always say, it's not *who* you are that's important but *what* you are. She has a very aggressive manner, quite unpleasant.'

I imagined that Mrs Jankiewicz had given Mrs Dudley one of her famous 'put-downs' and it had not been well received. There wasn't room for two such dominant personalities under one roof and I had no doubt that, formidable as Mrs Dudley was, she had met her match at last.

Bidding Mrs Dudley a brisk farewell I went off to hear Mrs Jankiewicz's side of the encounter, looking forward eagerly to telling Rosemary all about it.

CHAPTER SEVEN

The following week my son Michael came home for the summer vacation with two suitcases of washing, a heavy cold and a copy of *The Good Beer Guide* with every pub within a radius of fifty miles of Taviscombe hopefully marked in red. This meant that a large proportion of my life for the next few days was spent in the kitchen making hot lemon and honey and mounds of chilli con carne ('Feed a cold, Ma, and starve a fever') to the relentless hum of the washing machine.

'Is there any more news of Mrs Rossiter?'

We were sitting out in the garden drinking home-made lemonade.

'No, I'm afraid not. Things seem to have come to a standstill. There's been no sign of her, dead or alive. There's nothing more the police can do—or anyone else, for that matter. It's just an extraordinary mystery. I can't help worrying. Is she hurt or ill, or in some sort of difficult or dangerous situation?'

'I hope she's all right, she was a nice old bird. I liked her.' Michael fished a lemon pip out of his glass and flicked it into the flower border. 'She was very kind to me. Do you remember when I had measles? She came and read to me every day, for hours. I think we worked our way through the whole of the Jennings books!'

'She loved children; it's a thousand pities she has no grandchildren. I think the happiest time of her life was when Thelma was a very little girl.'

'Before she could talk, you mean!'

It really did seem as though Mrs Rossiter had vanished from the face of the earth. Michael reported that Thelma had telephoned one morning while I was out shopping to see if I had heard anything. I was quite glad to have missed her. After our last conversation I didn't feel very inclined to talk to her.

'Very tra-la, she was,' Michael said. '"Now *do* tell me how you're getting on!"' he continued in a passable imitation of Thelma's affected drawl. '"And don't you just *love* being in London after the dreary provinces? *Such* fun being where it's all at! You *must* come and have dinner with us one evening and meet some really *fascinating* people!" Yuck.'

'Don't you want to be where it's all at?' I asked, laughing.

'If it's where Thelma Douglas is, then no

thanks!'

Tris and Tessa, excited by our laughter, rushed round in circles barking, until Michael got up and began to chase them round the garden. I gathered up the glasses and went back into the house. As I stood by the kitchen window, watching Michael throwing a ball for the dogs, I thought once again about Mrs Rossiter's disappearance. A sudden thought struck me: Annie Fisher. Surely she must be very distressed, wrapped up as she was in Mrs Rossiter, yet I hadn't heard a word from her. I would have expected her to be on the doorstep straight away, questioning me in that fierce way of hers. Mrs Wilmot hadn't mentioned seeing her, either. Come to think of it, I couldn't remember having seen her around in the town lately. In a small place like Taviscombe you run into most of the people you know pretty often, in the two main streets, the supermarket or the post office, but I hadn't seen Annie since the time we had met in the library and that was before Mrs Rossiter disappeared.

Michael came back in from the garden to find me scrabbling through the pages of the telephone directory.

'Who are you looking for?'

'Annie Fisher.'

'You mean that person who used to be with Mrs Rossiter? Woman who looked like a frog?'

'A frog?' I looked up from the directory.

115

'Yes, I think you're right. Though perhaps we're influenced by the name—Fisher, Jeremy Fisher, Beatrix Potter—still, perhaps that's why I've never really liked her.'

'But you like frogs, Ma.'

'As frogs, not as people. Now you've interrupted me and I've lost my place. There seem to be an awful lot of Fishers.'

I finally found Annie's number—I remembered that she was living in a council flat down in Meadow Gardens—and decided to ring her. I dialled the number and stood waiting while it rang out. Foss came in through the cat door and began weaving round my feet in a determined way that meant he wanted food.

'In a minute, Foss,' I said as the phone went on ringing. When I finally convinced myself that no one was going to answer, I put down the phone and went to open a tin.

*   *   *

The next morning, after I'd finished my shopping, I needed to photocopy an article in a learned journal and to get to the one and only photocopier in Taviscombe I had to go past Meadow Gardens. On an impulse I turned down the road and began looking for number 9A, which was where Annie Fisher lived.

It was, I found, the ground floor flat in a house that had been divided into two. I went up the garden path, noticing as I did so that the grass needed cutting and the flower beds were full of weeds. That certainly didn't seem like Annie. When I got to the door I realised that the ground floor was empty. There were curtains certainly but, as I stepped off the path and peered in the windows, I saw that the rooms were bare of furniture. I opened the side gate and went through into the back garden. Here, too, the weeds were beginning to take over. Annie must have been gone for several weeks. I looked into a garden shed and saw nothing there but a couple of old bottles that had once held weedkiller or fertiliser and a rusty watering can without a rose. A voice behind me made me turn round quickly and in some confusion.

'She's been gone well over a month now.'

The woman next door was in the garden pegging tea towels on to her rotary clothes drier. She regarded me with interest but not surprise.

'Miss Fisher, that is, if you're looking for her.'

She was an elderly woman with tightly permed grey hair and a cheerful manner. I went over to the low fence that divided the gardens and said, 'Yes, I don't seem to have seen her around lately and I wondered how she was. But where is she? I'd no idea she was thinking of moving.'

'Australia.'

'Australia!' I echoed stupidly, as if I'd never heard of the place.

'Yes. Like I said, she's been gone over a month now. The council haven't let her flat yet. Well, it needs quite a bit doing to it, decorating and suchlike.'

'But—' I found it difficult to take in the fact that Annie wasn't there.

The woman regarded me with some concern. 'Was she a friend, then? You look like you've had a bit of a shock.'

'Yes, in a way. I've known her for years, since I was a child. It just seems so odd that she didn't mention this when I saw her last.'

The woman picked up the plastic bowl that had held her washing and said, 'Do you fancy a cup of coffee? I was just going to make one. I'm Mrs Taylor, by the way. It'd be nice to have a bit of company. I miss having Annie around; she often used to have a cup with me about now.'

'That would be kind,' I replied. 'My name is Sheila Malory. As I said, I've known Annie for ages and it *was* a bit of a shock to find she's suddenly gone away!'

I went round to the front and into Mrs Taylor's flat. She ushered me into the small sitting room which was crammed with furniture and a multiplicity of framed photographs and ornaments.

'Please do sit down,' she said. 'I'll just go and put the kettle on.'

I looked around at some of the photographs. In pride of place was a large framed studio portrait of a girl in cap and gown holding a rolled-up diploma. She had the same cheerful expression as Mrs Taylor and I assumed it was her daughter. Next to it was one of a man in a fireman's uniform and next to him a young man in a striped shirt, holding a football.

Mrs Taylor came back into the room with two cups of coffee and a plate of bourbon biscuits on a tray.

'There we are, then,' she said. 'Do you take sugar?'

I declined the sugar and accepted a biscuit. Mrs Taylor sat down opposite me.

'Well, now, about Annie,' she began. 'You know she had this brother who lives in Australia? Adelaide, it is. I was always interested, you see, because my Janet and her husband Roy, they went out to Perth—that's Western Australia. They've done very well. Janet's a teacher and Roy, he works for a chemical firm. They've got a lovely home! I went out to visit them last year, just after Jack died.' She indicated the photograph of the fireman. 'But anything about Australia's interesting, isn't it, when you've got someone out there? I always watch the Australian serials on the telly. Well, it shows you what it's like there, doesn't it? Anyway, this brother of Annie's—Sam he's called, but you'd know that—he's been out in Adelaide for years. He came over to pay Annie a visit, and before you could say knife he'd persuaded her to go back to Australia with him! Well,' she lowered her voice, 'from what I heard, his wife had left him and the daughter, too. So you can imagine, he saw Annie here all alone and thought she might just as well be looking after him!'

From her tone I gathered that she hadn't taken to Sam Fisher.

'But how on earth did he persuade her?' I asked. 'She was so very settled over here. She was always in and out to see Mrs Rossiter—that's the lady she used to work for. She's in a nursing home now. I can't imagine that Annie would ever have left her.'

'Oh yes, Mrs Rossiter. Annie was always on about her—how it was in the old days in that big house with all the other servants, and how Mrs Rossiter relied on her for everything. But you see, her brother got Annie interested in this religious thing. I can never remember which they are; not the Jehovah's Witnesses, the others, you know the ones I mean. Apparently they've got missions (I think that's what they call them) all over the world, here and in Australia. Well, Sam Fisher's one of them— one of the high-ups over there, according to Annie—and when he was here, the time before last, he got Annie to go to the meetings (they have them in Taunton) and she went on going after he went back to Australia. She went regularly, every week. Thursday afternoons she always used to take the bus into Taunton. Well, if it made her happy! It takes all sorts, doesn't it?'

'So that when Sam Fisher came over this time he persuaded her that she ought to go back with him ...'

'Said it was her Christian duty.' The words rang some sort of bell but I couldn't think what it was. Mrs Taylor continued, 'Just wanted to make a convenience of her, if you ask me, but she was very taken up with this religious thing lately.'

'Did she tell Mrs Rossiter that she was going?'

'Oh yes, she and that brother of hers took the old lady out for the afternoon in a car he'd hired and told her then.'

'Was she upset, do you know?'

'Well, Annie didn't say. She was so taken up with all she'd got to do before she went—going in such a rush like that. But *he* said she might as well go back with him; afraid she might change her mind, I shouldn't wonder. Sold all her things, just like that! I don't know how she could do it. I could never get rid of all my bits and pieces.' She looked around the crowded room. 'It was difficult getting it all in when I had to move in here, after Jack went, but I couldn't part with my treasures. Annie, though, she didn't seem to give a backward glance. She was a changed woman, you might say! It's funny—you think you know someone

121

quite well and then they go and do something you'd never imagine!'

'It's strange about Annie and Mrs Rossiter, though,' I said.

'Well, there was one funny thing. I didn't pay much attention to it at the time, but now you come to mention it...'

'What was that?'

'Well, I was having a cup of tea with her one day, after she'd told me she was going to Australia, and her brother was there. He was always around, I never really got the chance to have a proper talk with her before she went. Anyway, she was saying something about the old days, when she was with Mrs Rossiter, and apparently her brother used to work there too...'

'Yes, he used to be the gardener.'

'That's right. Well, she was saying how pleased Mrs Rossiter had been to see Sam and how interested she was in all this mission work he was doing in Australia and, instead of sitting there looking pleased with himself, like he usually did when she was going on about how marvellous he was, he shut her up. Just like that. "Mrs Taylor doesn't want to hear about that," he said. Well, he was quite right, I didn't! But it *was* a bit odd, though. He gave her quite a look and changed the subject.'

'How strange.'

'To be honest with you, Mrs Malory, I didn't take to him, not at all. There was something there that I didn't like. I can't put my finger on it, but you know how it is with some people...'

'To be honest, I've never really liked him myself, but Annie seems very fond of him and I do hope she is happy out there in Australia. It's a big step to take at her age.'

'I can't say I'd fancy living so far way, myself. It's a beautiful country and when I went out there our Janet said to me, "Why don't you stay on here, Mum?" I know they'd really like me to make my home with them, but I couldn't live anywhere but England, could you?'

'No, I don't believe I could. Did Annie leave you an address in Adelaide?'

'Yes. Just a minute, I'll get it for you.' She got up and rummaged through some papers in a drawer. 'Here it is.'

I copied the address in my diary and thanked Mrs Taylor for the coffee.

'It was nice having a bit of company. You get lonely sometimes when your family has gone away. My boy Paul—that's him in his football things—he's in the Navy now. Married a very nice girl and they've got two lovely little boys, but they live down in Cornwall so I don't get to see them very much. I can't manage the journey on my own now. It's a dreadful thing to get old, isn't it? Still, we should count our blessings and make the most of what we've got. At my time of life every day's a bonus, that's what I always say!'

Mrs Taylor was still in full flow as I waved goodbye and walked down the path to my car. I felt a pang of sadness for her, as I did for my Meals on Wheels regulars who, I always felt, had more need of a sympathetic listener than meat and two veg.

My way back from Meadow Gardens lay through the hinterland of guest-houses and bed-and-breakfast places that led down to the sea. The larger, grander ones had names to match—like Balmoral, Deeside or Glendower and the smaller houses, now at the height of the season with No Vacancies signs proudly displayed, had names that were more romantic or fanciful—Lorna Doone Cottage, Simla, Verona or even Valhalla. I looked, as I always did, for one small house, relic of a more innocent age, whose gate bore the legend 'Gaydaze'. The narrow roads were difficult to negotiate since cars belonging to the summer visitors were parked on either side, so I turned off and went along the promenade and round by West Lodge. As I did so I suddenly remembered why the words 'Christian duty' had rung a bell. It was the phrase Ivy had heard the unknown man using to Mrs Rossiter.

As I unpacked my shopping I told Michael what I had found out in Meadow Gardens.

'And Ivy—you must go and see her while you're home this time, darling. It would mean so much to her—did say something about a mission or missionaries.'

124

'So you think that the mysterious stranger might be Sam Fisher?'

'Well, if he's been living in Australia for some time, I suppose he might have an accent. Ivy did say that he sounded like a foreigner.'

'And he was trying to get money out of Mrs R.?'

'He's just the sort of man who would and especially now, if he belongs to one of those odd religious sects. They always seem to be able to get money out of old ladies. And that would explain why he shut Annie up when she was telling Mrs Taylor about him talking to Mrs Rossiter about his mission.'

'I say! Do you think Annie and Sam Fisher have taken Mrs Rossiter off to Australia with them?'

'Don't be ridiculous.'

'But think about it, Ma. You said she was pretty miserable in that bin she was in. She may have felt that *anywhere* would be better than that.'

'It's not a bin, it's a perfectly respectable nursing home. And anyway, she'd never do such a thing.'

'Why not? She's used to Annie and she trusts her. And you said yourself how persuasive these people are.'

'But *Australia*!'

'It's not the other side of the moon—people do go there.'

'Yes, but...'

'It all fits in. Why she didn't say anything to anyone. Well, she'd know they wouldn't let her go, so she pretended she was just nipping into Taunton to do some shopping and then Annie and Sam were waiting for her...'

'The man and woman Ed Cooper saw!' I told Michael about my conversation with Ed.

'Well, there you are then! I wonder if her passport's gone. Is there any way you could find out?'

'No, really, Michael. It simply isn't possible...'

'And didn't you say that she'd been in a funny sort of mood?'

'According to Mrs Jankiewicz, yes. Oh, I don't know. The whole thing is so fantastic, so far-fetched.'

'But possible?'

'Well, yes. I suppose so. I *suppose* I'd rather she was in Australia with Annie and her brother and that religious set-up than lying dead in a ditch somewhere in the Quantocks, but still...'

I found it difficult to accept such a bizarre solution to the problem, though I had to admit that no one had come up with a better answer. We argued round in circles for some time until I suddenly realised that it was nearly one o'clock and the chops I'd bought for lunch were still lying uncooked on the work-top.

126

CHAPTER EIGHT

The days slipped imperceptibly away, as they always seem to do in the summer. Michael went off for a week to stay with some friends in Dorset and I decided to seize the opportunity to get some work done. I had several books for review and the deadline was fast approaching. So I shut a protesting Foss in the kitchen with the dogs (he has a habit of trying to play duets with me on the typewriter keys) and began to type a fierce condemnation of yet another study of Charlotte Brontë. The author was one of those earnest, humourless so-called scholars whom my friend Alison compares to snails leaving their slimy tracks all over English literature, who wrench the life and work of the poor author to fit their own idiotic theories. This particular study was written in a turgid pseudo-psychological jargon that seemed to have no connection with the very real woman who had lived, felt, thought and written in nineteenth-century Yorkshire.

For a while my irritation drove me fluently on, but when the momentum slowed down and I was at a loss for a suitably biting phrase I looked up from my typewriter and gazed out at the garden (as I often do) for inspiration. A strange sight met my eyes. An extremely large bird was walking along the garden path, strolling you might almost say, its head on a long, elegant neck, turning from side to side, as if admiring the flowers. I was irresistibly reminded of an Edwardian lady graciously complimenting her hostess on a fine display of delphiniums. It walked along one path, then turned and completed the circuit of the garden. Its size and the graceful way it moved made it seem like some mythical, fabulous creature. I stood up to get a better view and the movement must have startled the bird because it rose in the air and flapped away. Only when I saw the spread of its great wings did I realise that it was a heron, attracted by the stream that runs round the garden, taking time off from its hunting to have a little stroll for pleasure.

I was still feeling slightly bemused, almost unreal, when the telephone rang.

'Sheila?'

It was Thelma's voice, peremptory as usual, putting me, as always, slightly on the defensive.

'Sheila, have you seen or heard anything of Alan?'

'Alan?' I repeated stupidly.

'My brother. Alan.' She spelled it out as if for a backward child.

'No. Why on earth should I?'

'He's disappeared and I wondered...'

'Disappeared?'

'Oh, for goodness' sake, Sheila, stop interrupting and listen!' Her voice was shriller than usual and what Michael calls its smarmy

128

quality was missing. 'I've just had a telephone call from the Ecology Centre in Harare. He went off to this conference in Bristol six weeks ago and hasn't been heard of since. He did go to the conference—they checked that—but then he just vanished into thin air.'

'How extraordinary!'

My feeling of unreality deepened.

'It certainly is. First Mummy and now Alan!'

'When did you last hear from him?'

'Well, that's it. I had a phone call from him a couple of months ago and he sounded—well—rather strange.'

'In what way?'

'Not like himself at all. Very excited, all strung up. He gabbled away—I could hardly get a word in edgeways.'

'That doesn't sound like Alan.'

Alan had always been the quiet one, a silent, sulky, sullen little boy. He had been sent away to school when he was seven, glad, even at that age, to be out of his father's way, out of reach of his temper. Mrs Rossiter grieved for him but even her love didn't seem able to reach him. He spent the holidays at home keeping out of the way of an irascible father and a sister who noticed him only when she wanted something to tease and torment. Yet I found it difficult to be sorry for him. He was the sort of child who would whine and complain if he thought he could get you into trouble with the grown-ups;

there was something curiously unlovable about him. It had always seemed so unfair that Mrs Rossiter, who had so much love to give, should have been surrounded by such an unloving and unlovable family.

'No, well, it seems that he had met this woman. She's some sort of journalist, an American—you know the type, hard-bitten, very much a woman of the world. Anyway, it seems that she was getting up an expedition to go to South America, something to do with an ecological scandal. I don't pretend to understand such things—all a lot of nonsense, if you ask me. And Alan wanted to go with her. Honestly, Sheila, he sounded totally *infatuated*! So unlike Alan. I don't believe he's ever had a girl friend of any kind all his life. Gordon used to wonder if he was gay, but I said no, he simply wasn't anything...'

Infatuation, indeed, love of any kind, certainly seemed the last thing I would have expected of the Alan I remembered.

'So you think he's gone off with her?'

'Well, he said that they needed to raise quite a lot of money to finance the expedition and then, of course, there'd be all the organising to do. Anyway, he certainly hadn't told his Ecology Institute that he wasn't going back to Harare after the Bristol conference—he should have been back there a couple of weeks ago.'

'It does seem odd that they should both have vanished,' I said.

'Yes, I wondered ... Oh, bother. Look Sheila, I've got a very important call coming through on the other line. Anyway, it's difficult to discuss these things on the phone. Can you meet me for lunch in Taunton one day this week? I can't spare the time to come all the way to Taviscombe. Shall we say the day after tomorrow, one o'clock, at Cobblers? Will you book a table?'

Barely waiting for my reply, she rang off.

I reflected that it was typical of Thelma that she naturally assumed that nobody else's time was as valuable as hers and that everyone would fit in with her arrangements. For a moment I toyed with the idea of ignoring the whole affair but, as I knew I would, I found myself telephoning to book a table at the rather trendy wine bar Thelma had selected. Oh well, I told myself, it *was* rather strange and my curiosity was certainly aroused.

A furious and persistent yelling from the kitchen reminded me that Foss was bored with just the dogs for company and wished to be off on his own mysterious business. I let them all out into the garden and did a little brisk weeding to bring myself back to reality.

As I was wrestling with a vicious piece of convolvulus that had wrapped itself round an especially fine sweet william and was trying to choke the life out of it, I was trying to imagine Alan with some hard-bitten female American journalist. I pictured her with short blonde hair, a deeply suntanned face and bright blue eyes, like Hollywood's idea of a Hemingway heroine. She would be wearing a beautifully cut safari suit, have an expensive camera slung round her neck and drink Scotch on the rocks. What I *couldn't* picture was the nebulous figure of Alan at her side.

I did a lot of shopping in Taunton before I went to Cobblers (perhaps with a vague idea of establishing an independent reason for being in Taunton and not just falling in with Thelma's plans) so I was loaded down with parcels and glad to find that I was there first. I sank into my chair and disposed the parcels about my feet. The wine bar was quite full and to my surprise I found that the next table was occupied by six Roman Catholic priests, one of whom was in a splendid black soutane piped at the cuffs and hem in red, with touches of purple at the neck. It seemed a jolly party to judge from the bursts of laughter, helped, perhaps, by the fact that they appeared to be drinking five bottles of wine between the six of them. I was reminded of those splendid pictures of feasting Cardinals that used to hang in the dining rooms of country hotels when I was young. I was wondering idly about the priest in the soutane and his position in the hierarchy (the other priests, all more conventionally dressed, seemed very deferential) when Thelma arrived. Strangely enough she too was wearing ecclesiastical purple, a rather nice suit. I thought she was a bit old for such a fashionably short skirt, although I must admit that her legs have always been better than mine. She greeted me in her usual gushing way. We ordered our food and half a bottle of wine ('quite a robust little white') chosen by Thelma.

'You'll only want one glass, I suppose, if you're driving,' she said, 'and I must keep a clear head because I've got *masses* of work to do on the train going back.'

She told me about some of the deals she was engaged on, dropping names that she knew I would have heard of, and seeming quite composed, unlike her agitated manner on the telephone.

'Well,' I said, breaking in on one of her stories, 'what about Alan, then?'

She took a mouthful of her Coquille St Jacques before replying, as if she wanted a moment to collect her thoughts.

'He's really obsessed by this woman,' she said at last. 'He couldn't talk about anything else.'

'What sort of things did he tell you?'

'Oh, mostly how marvellous she was—all about the *scoops*'—she emphasised the word scornfully—'she's pulled off and how generally high-powered everyone thinks she is.'

'Is she in love with him?' I asked.

Thelma gave a contemptuous laugh. 'How could she be? You know Alan! No, I should think she's out for what she can get. Someone

133

must have told her about Mummy's money and she probably thought that Alan was rolling! Well, of course he isn't. Mummy gives him an allowance that's far too generous, really, I mean, what on earth can he spend it on in Harare! And she pays for that depressing flat in Earls Court. But he gets practically nothing from that Ecology place, so he hasn't the sort of money *she* would be interested in.'

'So what's the attraction for her then?'

'I imagine he's told her that he can get Mummy interested in financing this expedition, whatever it is.'

'Did your mother say anything to you about it? I mean, had he written?'

'No, but I don't think he would. I think he was planning to come and talk to her about it when he was over here for that conference. You know how silly Mummy was—the thought of seeing her little boy again after such a long time.' Thelma's voice was positively corrosive. 'I expect he thought it would be easy to wangle quite a large sum out of her.'

'She always liked to help people,' I said slowly, 'and she could be very easily influenced, but still, if it was a great *deal* of money—and such an expedition would cost a lot, I should think—well, she might have hesitated. She would probably have wanted to consult Mr Robertson.'

'That old fool!' Thelma interjected almost automatically, but she went on more

134

thoughtfully, 'Yes, you may be right, she could be stubborn sometimes. *I've* found that.'

Anyone contradicting Thelma, however mildly, was always stigmatised as stubborn.

'So *that* might be the explanation. The little *bastard*!'

Thelma suddenly looked so furious that I was completely taken aback. Her dark eyes were blazing—they seemed to grow in size, dominating her face, as they did when she was a child in a tantrum at not getting her own way.

'Explanation of what?' I asked nervously, half-expecting that she would turn on me as she used to do when she was thwarted or frustrated. With an effort she pulled herself together and spoke quite coolly.

'I'm sure he met Mummy here in Taunton, got her alone—took her for a drive, perhaps—asked her for the money and then, when she refused, he disposed of her somehow.'

'For God's sake, Thelma!'

My exclamation must have been very loud and vehement because the priests at the next table all stopped talking and looked at me curiously. I lowered my voice and repeated, 'For God's sake, she's his mother!'

'Oh, he probably didn't mean to *hurt* her, but he does have that terrible temper.'

'But even so . . .'

'Remember Marigold?'

I was silent. Certainly I remembered Marigold. She was the pony Alan had had

135

when he was about ten years old. One day I had been sent out with Thelma to find Alan and tell him to come in to lunch. He was in the paddock where some jumps had been set up—his father had some idea of entering him for a local gymkhana and Alan was required to practise for several hours every morning.

As we approached, Thelma, who could never resist taunting her brother, made some scathing remark about how feeble his riding was and what a fool he would look at the gymkhana. Alan's face darkened with anger, since riding was the one thing he did reasonably well. He pulled the reins tight, wheeled the pony round and put her at one of the jumps. He had hauled her round angrily and clumsily and the poor creature knew that she was wrong-footed for the obstacle so she sensibly stopped and refused to jump. In a frenzy now, Alan jerked at her head and kicked her forward, but she wouldn't budge. Her ears were back and her eyes were rolling. He lashed at her with his whip, again and again, screaming incoherently, almost hysterical by now. Thelma was laughing; she seemed to be enjoying the spectacle. Horrified, I rushed forward and tried to seize the whip, but Alan brought it down on my shoulders. Furious with the pain I snatched at it again and managed to wrench it away from him and somehow pulled him off the pony. He lay where he fell, beating the ground with his fists and screaming. Ignoring him, I tried to soothe the terrified pony and led it away to find the lad they employed as a groom, who bathed the deep weals on the pony's flank and told me that it wasn't the first time such a thing had happened.

I was so upset and furious at the hurt to the pony that, forgetting my fear of Colonel Rossiter, I marched straight into his study and told him what had happened. He didn't say a word but strode past me and sent Alan off to his room. I don't know what was said, but quite soon afterwards Marigold was sold and Alan didn't ride again.

'But surely—he was only a child—hasn't he outgrown that terrible temper?'

'Oh, he keeps it under control, mostly. Well, you know how *wet* everyone thinks he is, but there have been incidents. There was one in India, that was why he left that UNESCO project there. Oh, it was hushed up of course, otherwise they wouldn't have taken him on in Africa, but Mummy told me about it. She'd paid a lot of money in compensation and she was very worried, as you can imagine.'

'But even so, what you are suggesting is just too impossible!'

'You didn't hear how utterly *obsessed* he was with this woman. Honestly, Sheila, this is the only big thing that has ever happened to him in his entire life and if he thinks that Mummy's money is the only way he can get her, then I

137

don't think he would let anything—and I do mean anything—stop him.'

I drank the last of my wine. I felt that I needed some sort of restorative after Thelma's extraordinary suggestion.

'Is there any way you can find him?' I asked.

She shrugged. 'The world is a big place. He could be anywhere, just waiting for his inheritance.'

'What will you do?'

She was silent for a while and then she said, 'There's not much I can do. I don't suppose we will ever be able to prove it. I might ask Simon what he thinks.'

'Simon?'

'Our lawyer.'

'Oh yes, you told me about him. A charmer, I think you said.'

She smiled. 'Yes, he most certainly is that, but very, very bright as well. He's done so much for the business, I honestly don't believe we would have got where we are without him. Of course'—she leaned forward and spoke very confidentially—'he is reckoned to be one of the best contract lawyers on either side of the Atlantic.'

'Goodness,' I replied, somewhat taken aback by Thelma's change of tone after the amazing things she had been so recently discussing. 'He sounds very high-powered. How old is he?'

'In his thirties—his *late* thirties,' she said,

138

'and very *mature*. Quite an amazing range of experience. It will be invaluable to me in New York. I'm going over there soon for a couple of months; we're taking over the Burkhardt agency. I'm telling you this in confidence, of course.' She looked at me sharply, but then remembered who she was talking to and gave me her usual condescending smile. 'It really is the *big* one and I'm so excited about it.'

She certainly did look excited, but somehow it didn't seem to me like Thelma's usual animated account of her cleverness and success.

'How about Gordon? Is he going with you?'

'Goodness, no. Someone's got to stay behind and look after all the irons we've got in the fire over here. Anyway, he's no good with the Americans, not *together* enough!'

I was surprised. Usually everyone connected with Thelma was never less than perfect in every way, and she had been telling me for years just how clever Gordon was.

She leaned towards me again and spoke in the same confidential tone. 'Actually, Simon thinks that he *might* be able to do something about the Trust.'

'I thought a Trust was inviolate,' I said, remembering some of Peter's cases.

'Not if you're *really* clever. Of course we'll have to wait until Aunt Maud is dead, but that should be any day now, wouldn't you think? I must ring Marion and see how things are going. I'd like to get things moving before we go to New York.'

I was so disgusted at her hard and calculating attitude that I remained silent.

Thelma, of course, didn't notice my reaction and went on, 'If Mummy hasn't turned up—and I very much doubt now that she *will* turn up, don't you?—after a certain period then I gather that she can be assumed to be dead. I'm sure Simon can find a way of speeding things up. I expect it will cost a bit, but it will be worth it in the end. Actually, I thought that when we've wrapped things up in New York we might go to South Africa and see for ourselves what the situation is at the store in Pietermaritzburg. Mummy and Aunt Maud have had reports and things, but old Robertson and Aunt Maud's man in Inverness aren't exactly live wires! Simon always favours the hands-on approach to any problem...'

She took a lipstick and compact out of her bag, briskly outlined her mouth in dark red, swept a brushful of coral powder over her cheekbones and took an American Express Gold Card from her wallet.

'Well. Do let me know if you have any news; I rely on you to keep me posted about the Taviscombe end. They'll let you have my New York number if you ring the office.'

The waitress, a friendly girl in a long ochre skirt and a Cobblers T-shirt, brought the bill and Thelma stretched out her hand for it.

'No really,' I said. 'Let me at least pay my half.'

'I wouldn't *dream* of it.' Thelma gave me one of her saccharine smiles. 'It was so *sweet* of you to come all this way to have lunch with me. Anyway, I can charge it to expenses.'

I rose to my feet and began to gather up all my parcels.

'Good heavens!' she exclaimed. 'Whatever did you find to buy in *Taunton*?'

As we passed the table where the priests had sat, the girl in the ochre skirt was gathering up all the wine bottles. I reflected that they'd certainly had a much jollier lunch than I had.

CHAPTER NINE

When I got back from Taunton the phone was ringing just as I got to the door. I dumped all my parcels in a heap and fished frantically for my key, wrenched the door open and picked up the phone quite out of breath and rather annoyed, as one (unreasonably) is with the caller.

My annoyance evaporated when I heard Rosemary's excited voice.

'Jilly's had her baby. It's a girl. Seven and a half pounds. They're going to call her Cordelia Rosemary! Isn't it *marvellous*!'

'Oh, Rosemary, I'm so glad. Cordelia's a

charming name and you must be thrilled about the Rosemary bit.'

'Yes, wasn't it sweet of them! Cordelia's a bit of a mouthful, but I expect she'll end up as Delia.'

'How's Jilly?'

'Fine. It wasn't too bad, apparently. Roger rang me when it started. Luckily Mummy's still in West Lodge so I just got into the car and rushed straight off to Taunton. They've asked me to stay with them for a few days, just until Jilly's got herself sorted out. They send them home from hospital almost *immediately* nowadays, so the poor lamb's pretty nervous about coping on her own at first.'

'I'm not surprised! In our day they kept us in for ages—at least until we felt reasonably competent.'

'Jack's holding the fort at home, looking after the animals and so on, and Elsie will call in every day at West Lodge to see what Mummy wants fetching and carrying. But, I wonder, *would* you mind being an angel and popping in from time to time, just to see how she is? It's no good asking Jack; he always irritates her. Actually she'll be more disagreeable to him than ever, poor love, because he's got to tell her about the baby and—more important—that I won't be around for a week. I didn't have the nerve to do it myself. She's *not* going to be pleased.'

'Yes, of course I will. I'd have thought she'd

be thrilled to have a great-granddaughter. Something to boast about to all her chums.'

'Oh yes, *that's* okay, but she'll be furious that I won't be there to hear her tell me how much better children were brought up in *her* day, and various related topics!'

'I'll call in tomorrow and she can tell me, instead. Actually, I want to drop in there and see Mrs Jankiewicz. She hasn't been herself since poor Mrs Rossiter disappeared.'

'Poor soul, I expect she misses her. No news, I suppose?'

'No. I saw Thelma yesterday, actually.'

I didn't feel that this was the moment to tell Rosemary of Thelma's extraordinary theory about Alan.

'How was Horrible Thelma? As elegant as ever?'

'More so, if anything. A gorgeous purple suit with practically a *mini* skirt. Far too young for her, though she can carry it off, of course, because she's small and has that marvellous figure. She looked very Sigourney Weaver, very Wall Street. She's just off to New York with her glamorous young lawyer. Goodness! I've just realised!'

'What?'

'It's only just dawned on me. I do believe our Thelma is having a bit of a fling!'

'No!'

'It's this young lawyer, she just couldn't stop talking about him, and it was how she said his

143

name. You know.'

'Well! Fancy! Thelma, of all people!'

'Come to think of it, she sounded positively *coy*.'

'Did you say *young*?'

'She was a bit defensive about that. She said he was in his late thirties, which probably means he's about thirty-five.'

'And they're going to America together? What about Gordon?'

'Oh, *he's* staying behind to run things here. Definitely *not* wanted over there.'

'How fascinating! So you think she's really smitten?'

'The more I think about it, the more sure I become. I do believe it's love at last!'

'Gordon?'

'Oh, Gordon was a business arrangement, on Thelma's part at least. He owned the agency in the first place, I think, and anyway, he's quite a bit older than she is. No, I'm sure this is the real thing for our Thelma!'

'Well, do try and find out some more. Oh! That's Roger back from the hospital. I must dash and get him some tea. Thanks for coping with Mummy.'

'Give my love and congratulations to Jilly and Roger and find out what they'd like for little Cordelia. I never know what babies need these days.'

'I should think a large supply of disposable nappies! Bless you, I'll ring you soon.'

I put the telephone down, retrieved Foss, who'd darted out when I opened the door, released the dogs from the kitchen and let them welcome me. Then I gathered up my parcels and went upstairs.

As I tried on my various purchases and decided that I had been over-optimistic about several of them, which would have to go back to Marks and Spencer, I thought of Thelma in her purple suit—a new, youthful looking Thelma. Now I had decided that she was in love, various things fell into place. There was, as I'd told Rosemary, the tone of her voice as she spoke Simon's name, and the sort of happy glow she had when she talked about him. I'd never seen her like *that* before. And she had seemed less sure of herself, more human than I'd ever known her. And then there was the strange way she had accused Alan of their mother's murder and then almost dismissed it, as if she had something even bigger on her mind. Simon. Or rather, the irresistible combination of Simon and the possibility that he might be able, somehow, to break the Trust. Nothing else would have diverted her mind from that monstrous accusation.

The telephone rang just as I was wriggling out of a skirt that declared itself to be a size 16 but certainly wasn't. It was my friend Anthea to ask how many scones I would be contributing for the cream tea at the Red Cross Fête the next day. Since I'd forgotten all about it, I recklessly promised a couple of dozen and hurried down to the kitchen to make them.

As I too hastily sifted the flour (so that quite a bit went over the work-top and not into the basin) I began to think more clearly about what had seemed at first the preposterous suggestion that Alan might have killed Mrs Rossiter. It *was* just possible. He certainly was a strange person, and if Thelma was right that he was so obsessed by this American, then he probably would have asked his mother for money for the expedition. But could he really—even with his terrible temper out of control—could he really have killed her? I stopped kneading the scone dough and stood with my floury hands suspended above the basin, considering this appalling thought. If he had hit out, with some sudden gesture, an involuntary expression of rage ... Well, she was an old woman and quite frail; it wouldn't take a lot to kill her. Afterwards he would be horrified and frightened at what he had done, would have hidden the body somewhere.

Had it been Alan whom Mrs Rossiter met in Taunton that day? He might well have told her to keep their meeting secret, because he wouldn't want Thelma to hear about his asking for money. He knew his sister well enough to know that she would be only too eager to thwart him. A man and a woman, Ed Cooper thought he had seen in the car park. Was the American woman with him? Had she been implicated? Thelma hadn't told me her name, but she must know it. Could I find out where *she* was now and if Alan was with her?

I put one tray of scones into the oven and rolled out the second lump of dough. It's possible that Mrs Rossiter might—left to herself—have given Alan the money, except that she would have been too frightened of Thelma's furious reaction. Alan would have known this and, just as Thelma's taunts when he was a child had tipped him over the edge into mindless fury, so this knowledge might have had the effect of turning his rage on to his mother.

I dipped the pastry brush into the beaten egg and painted the tops of the scones carefully. It all made a sort of horrible sense if one allowed oneself to think about it in the abstract, as it were, not relating it to real people that one actually knew.

Tris and Tessa came into the kitchen and sat at my feet, fixing me with that concentrated gaze that usually compels me to gather up their leads and take them for a walk. I broke in half one of the scones that had risen lopsidedly in the baking and gave it to them. Tess ate hers in one gulp, as she always did, but Tris was not to be diverted and continued to exercise his will upon me, so that I took off my apron and went to fetch the dog-leads.

*　　　*　　　*

The Red Cross Fête was being held in the garden of a rather grand house on West Hill and as I hurried along the drive with my boxes of scones I was pleased to see that old Mr Sewell was now apparently quite recovered from his stroke and taking the money at the gate.

'You see,' he said, 'I told you I'd be back in harness before you knew it!'

'It's marvellous to see you,' I replied. 'How's Bijou?'

'Oh, she's very fit—just like her master!'

'Are there many people here yet?'

'Quite a few. The weather's not very good, I'm afraid, but'—he lowered his voice slightly—'everyone's curious to see Mrs Braithwaite's garden. She's always going on about it!'

I reflected that Mrs Braithwaite's garden would have to be absolutely perfect, for no weed, no untidy compost heap, no clutter of old flower-pots, however carefully hidden behind the potting shed, would escape the beady gaze of a dedicated fête-goer.

'I'd better get on with these, then,' I said. 'They'll be wanting them for the teas.'

I found Anthea and several other lady helpers methodically splitting scones, filling pots with cream and jam and conscientiously counting strawberries into small dishes.

'Sorry I'm a bit late,' I said.

'Better late than never, I always say.' Mrs

148

Burden, a plump, jolly woman wearing an apron that bore the legend 'Somerset—the Team to Watch', took my scones away and added them to others laid out on the trestle tables, where I hoped they'd be decently anonymous, since I feared they might be rather heavy. I was conscious that my mind had been on other things while I was making them.

I dutifully did the round of the various stalls, acquiring a pot of greengage jam, a couple of old Penguin thrillers and two pairs of knitted pink bootees for Jilly's baby. I guessed the weight of a cake (hopefully wrong, since it looked highly indigestible), won a bottle of Worcester sauce and not the Drambuie on the bottle stall and bought four raffle tickets for a prize the nature of which was not disclosed. Then, duty done, I made my escape.

It really wasn't a very nice day. There was a strong wind blowing off the sea and most of the holiday-makers were wearing anoraks with the hoods up as they wandered dispiritedly along the promenade. Some brave souls were eating ice-cream cones, but others were sensibly making for the Old Ship tea-rooms in search of a nice hot cup of tea.

Going into West Lodge out of the sharp wind I was quite glad of the wave of heat that met me, but after a few moments, as I climbed up the stairs to Mrs Dudley's room, I began to find the constant heat oppressive.

She was sitting in a chair by the window. Just

for a moment, when she turned towards me and before she recognised me, she seemed suddenly shrunk and frail. I felt a pang of something like pity, an emotion she had never inspired in me before. Then she greeted me in her old familiar manner and was herself again and the moment passed.

'Well,' I said, 'isn't it splendid news! A beautiful little girl!'

'I always think it's better if the first child is a boy,' she said. 'Though I suppose,' she added grudgingly, 'if there is no title or estate then it doesn't matter so much.'

'I'm sure you must be thrilled to have a great-granddaughter,' I said, trying to make it sound as if the achievement had been all hers.

'I can't say I greatly care for the name they have chosen. There have been no Cordelias in *our* family.'

'Oh, I think it's rather a pretty name,' I said, 'and it's out of Shakespeare,' I added placatingly.

'Indeed—and look what happened to *her*! I have always thought *King Lear* a quite shocking play, a terrible example of what happens to young people who do not pay proper respect to their parents!'

I mentally saved up this splendid piece of Shakespearean criticism for Rosemary and changed the subject.

'It will be nice for Jilly to have Rosemary with her for a few days. It's always difficult having to cope with a new baby at home, especially a first baby.'

'Rosemary does *far* too much for Jilly, I've always said so. She'll wear herself out.'

I suppressed a smile and said, 'Oh, I think she's enjoying it...'

'That's not the point. Jilly shouldn't think that her mother can just abandon her other responsibilities at a moment's notice. I wanted Rosemary to help Elsie give my bedroom a thorough spring-cleaning before I go home, and then there are the dining-room curtains, they need to go to the cleaners. And there are a hundred and one other things that really can't wait. Young people are so thoughtless and selfish these days.'

To divert her mind to other things I said, 'Well, you do seem to be nice and comfortable here.'

Mrs Dudley looked around her in a disparaging way. 'I really don't know if I can bear another fortnight in this poky little room. I must have a word with Mrs Wilmot. It is ridiculous that Mrs Rossiter's room is standing empty like that. It would suit me very well and it seems unlikely that *she* will ever use it again.'

'But we don't know...'

'I expect it was a road accident. People drive like lunatics these days.'

'But the accident would have been reported...'

'Hospitals are totally inefficient. When I

think how well the Taviscombe Hospital was run when I was with the Red Cross during the war! Matron used to say to me, "Mrs Dudley, if only my nurses were as efficient and well-trained as you are." Well, of course, we all knew that we had to do our bit to help the war effort. That was the Dunkirk spirit. Things will never be the same again.'

I made the sort of acquiescent noises that were all Mrs Dudley required from her listeners and she went on, 'Poor Mrs Rossiter, now, she was quite hopeless—couldn't even roll a bandage! We used to have working parties at the Manor. Your mother used to come, though, of course, that was in the old days before she became such an invalid. Mrs Rossiter was useless at organising things, so I simply *had* to take over. Colonel Rossiter ran the Home Guard—he was just too old for military service. He missed both wars, rather strange if you think of it. A disagreeable man, very disobliging and a very nasty temper. Rather like that boy of his.'

'Alan?'

'Yes. You must remember that dreadful incident when he had to leave his school.'

'No, I don't think I ever heard...'

'They hushed it up, of course. People in Taviscombe were never told the truth. Everyone thought he just left. Well, he was eighteen and wasn't going to university. But my cousin's boy was at the same school and *she* told me. He was *asked* to leave. I'm surprised you didn't know. After all, your mother was supposed to be such a close friend.'

She looked at me maliciously and I said rather stiffly, 'If Mrs Rossiter told my mother something in confidence then she wouldn't have told *anyone*, not even me.'

Mrs Dudley looked annoyed but decided that she would rather continue her gossip than take offence at my remark.

'Oh, yes, it was quite a scandal, I believe. The other boy was badly hurt. The headmaster had a dreadful job to persuade the parents not to take legal action. No, Alan always was a difficult boy, and what has he made of his life? Living on the other side of the world with all those poor Africans—I saw a documentary about them on television the other day and all I can say is I'm glad that neither of *my* children are out there! A dreadful place, nowadays. Of course when my husband's uncle was a District Commissioner in Tanganyika things were *very* different, but all Alan seems to do is fiddle about with wells and poor farmers.'

'I'm sure it's very valuable work,' I said.

'But hardly a *career*, not like Thelma. Now there's a girl who's really got on!'

'Yes, I suppose you might say that.'

'No question about it. I know she had all that Rossiter money behind her, and I suppose she'll have a great deal more if her mother is dead, but she has turned out to be a wonderful

153

businesswoman. She's really left you and Rosemary a long way behind!'

She laughed unkindly and looked at me sharply, to see if I would rise to her remark, but I simply said, 'Yes, she is certainly successful in business.'

I stayed a little longer and then thankfully escaped for a cup of tea with Mrs Jankiewicz. I listened while she told me once again about the Old Days on her grandmother's estate in eastern Poland, which was familiar and comforting, and made me feel as though I was listening to a short story by Chekhov.

*　　　*　　　*

The weather improved in the next few days, and I was able to get out into the garden at last to do a few jobs. I was tying up one of the climbing roses which had blown down in the wind when a loud barking made me realise that Don had arrived to clean the windows. He stooped to pat the dogs before he unloaded his ladders, slightly hampered by Tris and Tessa who ran round him excitedly in circles.

'Hello, Don,' I said, 'I didn't expect you today.'

'No, well, you see, Mrs Malory, I've got these contract jobs now with some of the hotels and so on, so I'm having to fit my regulars in where I can. I hope it's not inconvenient?'

'No, today's fine, carry on. Would you like a

154

cup of tea?'

'Wouldn't say no.'

Taking this as a form of assent I went in to put the kettle on.

As I was taking off my gardening gloves I was aware of a loud bellowing from my bedroom and resignedly went up the stairs. Foss was perched on the back of an armchair by the window, the ridge of fur on his back standing up and his tail puffed out like a bottle-brush. He was informing me at the top of his voice that there was someone outside the window looking in at him. I scooped him up and told him not to be silly.

Don pushed the window open and said cheerfully, 'I see the old moggie still doesn't like me doing the windows, then.'

I apologised for my cat's impolite behaviour and Foss, rigid with disapproval, allowed me to take him away.

Don likes a good gossip and I have long since resigned myself to the fact that this is the price you have to pay if you want to get things done around the house, so I sat down at the kitchen table, poured out two mugs of tea, pushed a plate of bourbon creams towards him and said, 'Well, Don, and how is the world treating you?'

'Can't complain, Mrs Malory. Now I've got these cleaning contracts—course, with the hotels it's more the summer; there won't be so much in the winter when the visitors have gone.

But West Lodge should keep me busy all year round.'

'Oh, you're doing the windows there?'

He stirred a spoonful of sugar into his mug. 'Terrible thing about the old lady!'

'The old lady?'

'That Mrs Rossiter, disappearing like that. Proper mystery, that was.'

'Yes, it's been very worrying for her family and all her friends.'

'A very nice lady, always liked a chat. I thought she was lonely in that place.'

'Well, of course, her family don't live in Taviscombe so they can't get to see her very often.'

'She saw her son, though, she told me. All the way from Africa he was coming. She was that pleased!'

I sipped my tea, which was too hot to drink, and said casually, 'When did he come? Did she say?'

'Couldn't rightly tell. She told me about it the last time I was there before she went. Let me see, she must have gone off about a week after that, so I suppose he must have come some time that week. I mean, if he'd come and found she'd gone off like that he'd have made a fuss, wouldn't he? And I didn't hear nothing about anything like that when I was there the next time. Very full of it, they was, and having the police there and everything. Didn't like *that*, Mrs Wilmot didn't. Well, she wouldn't, would

156

she?'

'Did Mrs Rossiter say if her son was visiting her at West Lodge, or was she meeting him somewhere else?'

'I don't think she—no, hold on, she said she was going to see him in Taunton. Said it would be more convenient for him. Though if he'd come all the way from Africa, it seems to me he could have just as well come on out to Taviscombe and not made his poor old mother go into Taunton to meet him!'

'Oh, I think she liked little outings. She used to take a taxi.'

We had a little further conversation about the iniquitous price of taxis and how, if a bloke could get a decent car, instead of an old banger, he could probably make a fortune, and then Don packed up his ladders, leaving me with nice clean windows and another piece to be fitted somewhere in the jigsaw.

On a sudden impulse I picked some roses from the garden and went to see Mrs Jankiewicz at West Lodge.

Mrs Jankiewicz, too, was sitting by the window, but erect and alert. Her room faced Jubilee Gardens but, although there was the usual brilliant floral display, I knew it was only an indistinct mass of colour to her. It seemed to me that she sat by the window not so much to see what was going on in the world outside as to *be seen*, so that passers-by would know that she was there and still keeping an eye on things.

While I put the roses in a vase (deep ruby red glass in a heavy, ornately wrought pewter holder) she gave me the latest news of Sophie.

'She works too hard, that girl. Taddeus should not allow it.'

'I think she enjoys her work,' I said.

'Is not the point. To be a doctor's wife is hard enough—I know it—but to be a doctor's wife and also a doctor with no wife is terrible.'

We had had this conversation many times before as well.

'How's Kasha?'

Mrs Jankiewicz's face softened. Her granddaughter was the one person in the world who could do no wrong.

'She sings, at school in the choir. She has voice like an angel. Zofia has sent me a tape. She sends me tapes now instead of the letters, now that my eyes are not so good.'

'What a marvellous idea. And you must send tapes to her. I'll help you make one, shall I? Sophie would *love* that. Let's see if your cassette player has a built-in microphone.'

'I do not understand. I can press the button to play, Zofia showed me how...'

'Oh yes, it's fine,' I said, looking at the cassette player that Sophie had bought for her mother before she went away. 'Next time I come I'll bring a spare tape and you can record a message for them all. It's a shame,' I went on, 'that Mrs Rossiter never had any tapes from Alan. She would have liked that.'

A sound rather like a snort came from Mrs Jankiewicz, but she said nothing.

'I gather he's been in England, though,' I said, putting the cassette player on a shelf and turning to look at her. 'And she went into Taunton to see him.'

Still there was silence.

'Did she?' I persisted.

'Yes,' Mrs Jankiewicz said finally. 'Yes, she did see him. But it would be better if she had not.'

'But why?'

'Is no good, that one. Not a good son. Always upsets his mother.'

'What happened?'

She turned her head and looked again out of the window.

'She was crying, when she came back.'

'Poor soul,' I said.

She moved in her chair and faced me again.

'You are a mother, Sheila, you know how nothing can hurt you like a child, when they do not care...'

'Alan always was a horrible person,' I said. 'What happened this time?'

'She went into Taunton to see him. He had a woman with him and they want money for some journey they would make. I do not understand what it was, but they want a great deal of money. First Alan was so sweet—you know how people are when they want something—and this woman so *charming*.

They all have lunch at the Castle Hotel, so expensive it is there, and they tell her all about this journey, whatever it is, and she was so interested and she say she would like to help. Then Alan tell her how much it is and she is worried—so much money. Not that she cannot afford it, but she has—what do you say? trustees and she is, anyway, nervous at so much. So she says she will ask these trustees and let Alan know what they say. And then he is *furious*—you know how he can be? He makes a scene and the people in the dining room were all looking at them. You know how Mrs Rossiter hates such things. The woman, she tries to calm Alan and eventually he apologises to his mother and she comes back here. But she is so upset. She cries when she tells me. She had looked forward so much to see him, but all he wants from her is the money. Is no love, no affection. She say, when she refuse him the money straight away, he look at her as if he hates her!'

'How terrible,' I said. 'And how unfair that she, who is so loving, should be treated like that. Did she speak to her trustees, I wonder? When did all this happen?'

'About a week before...'

'Before she went away. I wonder if she saw Alan again. Do you know?'

'She does not say.'

'I wonder if it was Alan she went to see that day she went off?'

160

There was a tap at the door and Maureen came in.

'Are you going into the dining room for your lunch, then, or shall I bring it here?'

Mrs Jankiewicz rose to her feet with some difficulty.

'I go to the dining room, I need to see Mrs Whipple. Her daughter, she has sold the house for her and I do not think that Mrs Whipple has had all the money from it that she should. You must go now, Sheila, but you will come and see me again soon. You are a good girl and they are beautiful roses.'

She took Maureen's arm and they began their stately progress along the corridor to the dining room.

I walked slowly out of West Lodge into the brilliant sunshine and took a deep breath of air, as I always did when I got out of there, to reassure myself that I was out in the real world again, that I was still (relatively) young and healthy and free to live my life as I wanted. But, as I walked through the gardens to where I had left my car, it occurred to me that not only had Mrs Jankiewicz not answered my question, but that she obviously had had no intention of doing so.

CHAPTER TEN

We had a wonderful burst of summer weather, several weeks when the sun shone every day and the idea of rain seemed unthinkable. I'm lucky because my garden never really dries out and, when he's home, Michael can usually be coerced into lugging watering cans about if there's a hosepipe ban. We were sitting in the garden drinking iced coffee after lunch—me idly glancing through the *Telegraph* and Michael leafing rather desperately through his law notes as term approached and, with it, exams.

Once upon a time I used to look first at the Engagements, then at the Weddings and Births. Now, alas, I turn straight to the Obituaries.

'Oh dear!' I exclaimed. Michael looked up. 'Mrs Rossiter's sister Maud has died. "Peacefully, at home," it says. Poor Marion, I must write to her.'

'What will happen about the Trust now, I wonder?' Michael said. 'It'll be a marvellous bonanza for her solicitors—it could run for years!'

'Oh, darling, you make it sound like *Bleak House*—Jarndyce and Jarndyce!'

'Well, I won't say that the law hasn't changed at *all* since Dickens's day...'

162

'Thelma thinks her clever young man might be able to break the Trust,' I said.

'It would take a helluva time and cost a fortune.'

'Well, there seem to be several fortunes up for grabs. I suppose Thelma will swing into action now. Oh dear,' I sighed. 'I *do* wish I knew what has happened to poor little Mrs Rossiter. It seems incredible that she should have just vanished off the face of the earth.'

'There are several people who might be better off. Or, at least, they *would* be better off if she were proved to be dead ... If someone has bumped her off, then it's strange they haven't produced the body so's they can get at the money.'

I thought for a moment. 'I suppose they might want to establish an alibi or something. Alan, for instance; he might want to get back abroad. I mean, he wasn't to know that Mrs Rossiter told Mrs Jankiewicz that she'd met him. He might have reckoned that no one would ever know that he was in England at all.'

'Mm ... He'd have to be pretty stupid to take that sort of a chance. Do you really think he's the one?'

'I don't know. I can't believe that anyone could murder their own mother.'

'Greek literature is full of matricide and patricide and, anyway, look at the Old Testament!'

'Yes, I know, but not in *life*. Certainly not

163

someone we actually *know*.'

'Actually, I'd back Horrible Thelma as a murderer any day.'

'Oh, darling, really!'

'Think about it.' Michael put down the large binder that contained his notes and leaned forward. 'From what you've told me, she's mad keen to get a large sum of money to expand that business of hers and—all right—she'd get a vast amount if she waited until her aunt *and* her mother died, but she might need a substantial sum *now* and she would inherit a fair bit from her mother, in any case.'

A sudden thought struck me.

'She *might* need it in a hurry. I do believe she's going to ditch Gordon and go off with this young man, Simon. I told you about him. Gordon's a bit dreary, but he's no fool in business. She'd have to buy him out of the firm!'

'There you are, then.'

'But—Thelma—no, honestly...'

But the thought squirrelled deeper and deeper in my mind. If Alan's infatuation with this American female gave him a motive for his mother's death, then what about Thelma and Simon? She was a realist and would have understood (as Alan in his turn had done) that her most powerful attraction for Simon was financial. The not-quite-suitable mini skirts and the extra gloss she had imparted to her appearance were all very well, but what

Thelma needed to catch (and, more important, to hold) Simon was a share in a very profitable business. And to buy Gordon out she needed a great deal—the sort of sum she could only hope to get after her mother's death.

'But what about the time she came here just after Mrs Rossiter went missing?' I asked, trying hard to keep hold of reality. 'Asking if I knew anything. She was very distressed.'

'Was she really, though? About poor Mrs R.?'

I thought of Thelma's calculating explanation of the Trust and how disgusted I had felt. I remembered her coldness and lack of affection for her mother all the years I had known her.

'But why did she call, then?'

'To see if you knew anything, of course. Presumably Mrs R. arranged to meet her in Taunton. Thelma probably told her not to mention it to anyone for some reason...'

'What reason?'

'Oh, I don't know. Perhaps Thelma told her mother that she was supposed to be somewhere else, at some boring conference she wanted to get out of...'

'It sounds a bit far-fetched!'

'Well, whatever. Mrs R. meets Thelma...'

'*And* Simon; Ed Cooper saw a man and a woman. And *that's* what she would have told her mother. Mrs Rossiter was such a romantic, she would have been thrilled that Thelma had met the love of her life at last and would have been dying to see him! But she'd understand that it had to be kept a secret, at least for the moment. Thelma would be taking a tremendous risk, but then she's always been one for taking risks.'

'But Mrs R. was very fond of you and she just *might* have let something slip. Thelma had to find out if she'd said anything to you.'

'And all that flouncing about at West Lodge was just acting?'

'Why not? Anyway'—Michael opened his folder of law notes again and laid them out before him on the garden table—'you know what they say about murder. Who stands to gain? On that count Thelma is the number one suspect.'

'Alan inherits as well. He has a motive, too.'

'Has he?'

'Well, you know he has. Thelma says ...' I stopped.

'Exactly. You've only got Thelma's word about all that.'

'But he's been here in England. Don told me that Mrs Rossiter said she was going to meet him in Taunton and Mrs Jankiewicz said that she was upset when she came back. And she told me about the American woman, too.'

'Never mind. It just means that you've got two suspects now instead of one.'

'I don't really want *any* suspects. The whole thing is too horrible to contemplate. Would you like some more iced coffee?'

'Oh, yes, please. And Ma'—Michael's voice took on a coaxing note that I knew well—'if you *could* spare the odd half-hour to hear my notes. I've read them over and over and they simply won't stick.'

I fetched some more coffee and picked up the folder resignedly. A piece of paper with verses scribbled on it caught my eye.

'What's this?' I read aloud:

> "The wise solicitor requires
> To know the gist of *Rouse-v-Squires*
> And also that renowned brain-teaser
> Quoted in *The Oropesa*.
> Of these twain, the legal meaning
> Is the New Cause Intervening.
> You'll also need a knowledge thorough
> Of *Lamb-v-Camden London Borough*
> (Which should not confuséd be
> With *Tate and Lyle-v-GLC*.)"'

'I have to do something to pound all those dreadful cases into my head.'

'I like this one:

> "A maxim based on cases plenty,
> *Injuria non fit volenti*,
> Means that should a man consent, he
> Gives away his right to sue
> (An injudicious thing to do)."

'You ought to put them all together in a little book and get it printed by one of those law publishers in Chancery Lane. I'm sure generations of law students would rise up and call you blessed!'

'I did another one this morning, it's much more fun than revising. Do you want to hear it?'

'Go on.'

'"All of tort is founded on
Donaghue-v-Stevenson:
If you'd plead on Negligence
(Or for the plaintiff or defence)
You must learn its weighty moral,
Treasure it like gold or coral.
Negligence you must know pat:
Negligence is where it's at.
Yeasty, fizzy, full of bounce—
Believe me, it's the tort that counts."'

I laughed. 'Oh dear, Pa *would* have loved that! Still, come along; what do you want to do? Landlord and tenant? Or inheritance?'

I opened the folder and we got to work.

*   *   *

The rest of the summer simply rushed by and Michael went back to London with a case of clean laundry and lots of ticked-off entries in his *Good Beer Guide*. I settled down to the usual autumnal tasks of making apple chutney with windfalls—the smell of boiling vinegar seemed to permeate the whole house—and washing summer clothes and putting them away in suitcases under the beds because there never seemed to be enough space in any of the wardrobes.

Apart from a few senior citizens on Special Offer Autumn Breaks, Taviscombe emptied of visitors and became a reasonable place to live in again. I met Rosemary in a strangely peaceful Woolworths and said, 'Isn't it lovely to have the town to ourselves again! No endless queues in the supermarket, no finding the shelves stripped of bread at weekends.'

'I know. It's been worse than ever this year. I wish I was rich enough to go to somewhere like Iceland all summer!'

'How are Jilly and the baby?'

'Marvellous. She's managing very well and dear Roger's so good, far better than Jack ever was. They came down last weekend, just for the day, to see Mother, who was beginning to make umbrage-taking noises.'

'I gather she's back home again now?'

'Oh, yes. I think the relief was mutual when she left West Lodge! She likes to make brief forays there, but while Mrs Jankiewicz reigns supreme she wouldn't go in there permanently.'

'How did they get on?'

'There was a sort of icy protocol. Throne

spake unto throne and all that sort of thing. But I think Mrs Jankiewicz had the upper hand. Her intelligence system is even better than Mother's and, being Polish, she has the advantage of pretending not to understand anything she doesn't want to hear. It infuriated Mother.'

I laughed. 'Yes, I'd back Mrs Jankiewicz against all comers, especially since she has a very highly developed sense of justice which gives her a moral superiority as well.'

'Still no word of Mrs Rossiter. I suppose? I gather Mrs Wilmot is still keeping her room free—another sore point with Mother. But it seems a very forlorn hope now. Poor soul, it really is terribly sad.'

'I miss her very much. I hadn't realised what a big part of my life she was. Childhood memories, I suppose, and her being such a friend of my mother...'

'Have you heard anything from Thelma?'

'I had a postcard of the Manhattan skyline, so I gather she's been in New York. But she hasn't been down here. Or, if she has, she hasn't been in touch with me.'

'What about the glamorous young man?'

'With her in New York, I imagine.'

'Goodness, what exciting lives some people do lead!'

'Oh, I don't know, I don't think it would suit me. Think of the strain of always having to look your best, even when you'd rather just *slump* and put your feet up!'

'You're right, of course, but I can't help feeling that there must be a happy medium. There really ought to be more to life than trailing round Woolworths trying to find where they've hidden what used to be called the haberdashery. I mean, should actually finding a card of hooks and eyes and some knicker elastic be the pinnacle of human achievement?'

I went home and tried to justify my own existence by doing some work—making a start on a paper I was supposed to be giving to the Victorian Society on Mary Cholmondeley's novel *Red Pottage*—but my thoughts kept straying. For some reason I couldn't get out of my mind the picture of Mrs Rossiter's room at West Lodge and her few remaining possessions: the desk, the footstool, the French clock, the watercolour and the ivory gazelle. No, the gazelle wasn't there any longer. Had it been stolen? Or had Mrs Rossiter taken it with her that day when she went to Taunton? And if so, why? Certainly she could have done. It was small enough to go into her handbag. But what would she have taken it *for*? Not to sell it, she didn't need the money. To give to someone, then? Not to Thelma, who would have asked for it if she'd wanted it, as she'd taken everything else she wanted when the Manor House was given up. Perhaps for Alan, then, since it might have African connections. But it wasn't the sort of object I could connect with

Alan—unless it was to pacify him after their previous, unhappy meeting. Mrs Rossiter was all too experienced in pacifying the irate, in making the first gesture, in giving way. Or it could have been a gift to his American friend.

Tris and Tessa burst in through the open french windows after a boisterous game in the garden and lay panting at my feet. Sighing, I got up to get their water bowls. As I tucked Tessa's ears into her collar so that she wouldn't trail them in the water, I thought that the gazelle might just as easily have been a gift for Simon, a sweet and affectionate gesture that would have been typical of her. But each of these theories meant that Mrs Rossiter had met either Thelma or Alan on the day that she disappeared and that she had been murdered by one of her own children.

In some agitation I walked up and down the room, the dogs looking at me curiously, as I tried, in a physical way, to shake off such ideas. They were too preposterous, too unthinkable, or, as my mind began to accept the possibility, too unbearable. What was the alternative? Who else could have killed her? Not Marion—I was utterly positive of that—or Van. That left Annie Fisher and her brother, and the possibility that they had persuaded her to go away with them to Australia. It would have to have been planned in secret because of Thelma, who would certainly have put a stop to it if she had known about it. Mrs Rossiter would have had to pretend that she was coming back from Taunton that day, but—and here a bit of the jigsaw seemed to pop into place—she had taken the gazelle with her because it was the only thing from her past life that was portable. I was so pleased with that thought that I found myself looking at the Fisher theory with something like approval. Yes, surely that's what had happened. No nonsense about matricide. Quite simply, Mrs Rossiter had decided that anything was better than living out the rest of her life at West Lodge, and Annie had at least shown her a kind of affection by her years of devotion. Perhaps Mrs Rossiter believed that Annie was the only person who had ever really cared for her. Soon, perhaps, word would come from Australia—she would need to have money transferred out there—and everything would be made clear.

Resolutely I wrenched my mind away from the problem and went back to my typewriter. The dogs, resting their heads on their paws, resigned themselves to an afternoon of sleep.

CHAPTER ELEVEN

We get only one post a day now. It used to be two, and my mother said that before the war there were four, the last one at nine o'clock at night. Still, it could be worse; at least the letters are actually delivered to the door and we don't have to have those hideous mail-boxes by the front gate like the Americans.

I was sitting idly wondering whether to eat the second slice of toast or give it to the birds when I heard the letters plop into the basket. The basket beneath the letter box is a legacy of the time when Tris was a puppy and each morning saw an exciting race into the hall to see who got to the letters first. He still rushes out when he hears the post but now he is content to sit looking up at the basket waiting hopefully for the letters to drop through the mesh on to the floor. He was in the hall this morning, but Tessa (I could tell from the strange sounds coming from the kitchen) was too busily occupied nudging her bowl around the floor in an attempt to reach the last crumbs of breakfast to join him as she sometimes does.

I took the post back to the dining room and poured myself another cup of coffee. It was a varied collection. There was a postcard of Delphi from my cousin Lorna, an invitation to a conference on Nineteenth-century Historical Novelists, a note from my optician to say that my new reading glasses were ready, and a letter from Michael. This last item was so unusual (he favours the telephone as a means of communication) that I pushed the others to one side half-read and tore it open.

Dearest Ma,

I Take Up My Pen to tell you about Something Very Odd Indeed.

To begin, as they say, at the beginning. I had to go to the Dark Tower (the Law Society Library to you) to look something up in *Tolley on Inheritance*—some Swine has made away with the College Library copy. As you know I hardly ever venture through those dreaded portals. Actually, I nearly didn't make it this time, because they don't let you in unless you're wearing a tie. Fortunately I remembered in time and nipped into that rather grand gents' outfitters just round the corner and bought myself a nice little striped number—I think it's the Brigade of Guards or something because the porter at the Dark Tower was quite civil for once and didn't even go through my tatty old briefcase with a fine-tooth comb as he did the only other time I ventured in there.

You know what libraries are like. I had to wait ages before they got Tolley for me and while I was waiting I leafed through the odd journal—not very riveting—the *London Gazette* (published by Authority, whoever *that* may be) doesn't seem to have any film reviews. It's mostly lists of bankruptcies, windings up of companies, lists of wills—general death and disaster, not much there of what you might call Good News. They have a list of people who've died and the solicitors acting for them and I was just casting my eye over them to see if Pa's old firm was doing any decent business these days when I came across an entry that read: 'Edith Mary Rossiter (née Westlock) died October 15th. Solicitors: Cowley, Grey and Thomas, Coleford, Glos.' It must be the same one, don't you think? But what on earth was she doing in Gloucestershire and with new solicitors, too!

Anyway, for what it's worth, there you are. Poor old Mrs R. I hope you manage to find out what happened. I suppose Messrs C.G. and T. will be in touch with Horrible Thelma—that is, if she didn't change her will—so you should hear why on earth Mrs R. ended up there on the edge of the world. Let me know—I'd like to hear the end of the story.

Better get on with some revision, I suppose—exams next week. Though first, since cousin Hilary's off gallivanting again, I must go down and feed Tish, Tosh and Tush.

Love from your Afft. Son, Michael

At first I couldn't take in what Michael's letter had said and I had to read it several times before I accepted the fact that Mrs Rossiter was undoubtedly dead. Coleford. The name rang a bell. Years ago when Peter and I stayed for a few days at Monmouth, we had driven through the Forest of Dean and I seemed to remember we stopped at Coleford to find a post office to buy some stamps for our postcards. A small town, workaday, unremarkable, with no noticeably picturesque features—I could think of no reason why Mrs Rossiter should have visited it.

And why should she have made a new will? At least I supposed it was a new one, since they were new solicitors. My thoughts flew to Thelma. If Mrs Rossiter had died nearly three weeks ago then presumably Messrs Cowley, Grey and whatever had got in touch with her by now. And if Thelma had been told about the will then she would now know the circumstances of her mother's death, so why hadn't she telephoned to tell me about it? Of course, if she *hadn't* been left anything in a new will, then she might not have heard anything at all.

I got up from the table and went to get my handbag. As I rootled about in its depths to find Thelma's card with her office telephone number, I wondered briefly and maliciously what Thelma would do if she *had* been cut out of her mother's will.

I dialled the number and was put through to Thelma's secretary—no, Personal Assistant—whose bright efficiency made me stumble over my enquiry.

'Mrs Douglas isn't here right now. Can I help you?'

'It's a personal matter,' I said rather stiffly.

'When will she be back?'

The voice relented slightly and became more human. 'Well, actually, Mrs Malory, she's had to go back to New York. She'll be there for about six weeks.'

'When did she go?'

'Nearly a month ago.'

'I see.'

Thelma could have gone, then, before the solicitor's letter arrived. But Gordon would surely know something.

'Can I speak to Mr Douglas, then?' I asked.

'I'm so sorry, Mrs Malory, but he's in Milan and won't be back until next week.'

'I see. Oh well, it will have to wait until Mrs Douglas is back, then.'

'I've made a note of your call, Mrs Malory, and Mrs Douglas will have it the moment she gets back. Meanwhile if there's anything I can do, please do ring on this extension and ask for Trish.'

So I was no further forward. All day I turned over in my mind theories, some prosaic, some wildly fantastic, as to how Mrs Rossiter had ended up in Coleford. By the evening I knew what I was going to do. The very next day I was going to Coleford to find out somehow how Mrs Rossiter had died.

I rang Michael and told him what I had decided. 'I know the solicitors won't be able to tell me anything about her affairs,' I said, 'but surely, if I explain the very unusual circumstances, they might give me an address or something.'

'If it's quite a small firm,' Michael said, 'and if you can find a young assistant solicitor who's still wet behind the ears, and you do your middle-aged female in distress act, then I daresay you might get something out of them.'

'Well, Thelma and Gordon are both away and goodness alone knows where Alan is, so I'm practically next of kin. Anyway, I'll have a good poke around while I'm there. Who knows what may turn up.'

'Good luck. And Ma'—Michael hesitated and then said, 'do be careful, won't you? After all, she did disappear in very strange circumstances, so what I'm saying is, don't take any chances.'

'No, of course not. You know me.'

'I know what you're like when your curiosity's aroused. You just go plunging in.'

'I'll be careful. You go back to your work. What is it tonight?'

'A little light consumer protection and then a bash at company law.'

'Poor you. Have you had anything to eat?'

'I've just had an enormous pizza so you may set your mind at rest. Good luck with your sleuthing. Report back.'

* * *

The next morning was one of those brilliantly

fine late autumn days. I got up very early and left a lot of food for Foss. Packing some biscuits and water for the dogs and putting them in the back of the car, I set off as soon as it was reasonably light. Because I had left so early, of course, I ran into the Bristol morning rush-hour at the Almondsbury intersection of the motorway and there was a longer than usual wait to get on to the Severn Bridge. I always hate driving across long suspension bridges and keep looking nervously at the fragile-looking supports. Safely across and past the first road signs in Welsh, I felt that I had come a very long way (right into another country, in fact) so that I really deserved a break for coffee in Chepstow. I parked in the Castle car park and stood for a while looking at the noble ruin towering above me, perched on an eminence, keeping watch over the steep, muddy banks of the river below.

Working on the principle that wherever there is an ancient monument there is usually a café, I was delighted to find the Belvedere Tearooms just across from the car park. It was, I was glad to see, an old-fashioned, traditional teashop with small, slightly rickety tables and wheelback chairs, willow-pattern china and a large table at one end on which were laid out plates of very home-made looking cakes. I sat down at one of the tables and looked about me. I had been slightly surprised to find it open out of the season, but now I saw that it was full of locals and was obviously their morning meeting-place. A middle-aged woman, rather surprisingly wearing a hat, brought me coffee and a selection of cakes. After careful consideration I chose a rather chewy date and walnut slice, which seemed less rock-hard than the others on offer. But the coffee was very good and I was drinking it gratefully when a voice behind me exclaimed, 'Good Heavens! It's Sheila Prior!'

I turned and saw a large, round-faced woman in a tweed suit who certainly looked familiar. I was also conscious of a slight sinking of the heart, though I didn't know why. I was groping for a name to put to the face when she said, 'Ruth Barnes—though I'm Ruth Gibson now.'

'Of course!'

I knew now why my heart had sunk. Ruth Barnes had been our college bore. A nice girl. Good-natured. But terribly boring.

'Ruth!' I cried, trying to look delighted. 'What a surprise! Do you live here?'

'We do now. My husband retired last year and we moved here from London. We always *loved* the Forest—what? oh, the Forest of *Dean*, but we all call it the Forest. We used to come here for holidays when the children were small.'

She rattled on, just as she used to in the old days, pausing only to allow the odd murmur of (assumed) interest, about her husband (a civil

181

servant—Ministry of Transport) and her children (one a vet and one a mineralogist) and the house they had bought ('a converted coach-house, just *outside* Chepstow, Tutshill, actually') and the garden ('really too big for Arnold to manage on his own, but so difficult to get any sort of *reliable* help nowadays') and her own life ('desperately busy, but oh so *fulfilling*, if you know what I mean').

I had taken a bite of my date and walnut slice, which effectively gagged me so that I couldn't have uttered even if I'd been able to get a word in. But finally the spate of words slowed down and Ruth said, 'And what about you? Whatever brings you to Chepstow? How long are you here for?'

'Oh, I'm just passing through,' I said hastily. 'I'm on my way to Coleford.'

Typically she didn't ask why I was going to Coleford but continued her monologue. My old technique for dealing with Ruth came back to me automatically: I closed my mind to her conversation, allowing only the occasional phrase to penetrate, and continued to deal with the date and walnut slice.

'So many things you must look at in the Forest ... the Speech House ... the locals ... so quaint and odd ... very inbred, of course ... typical border country ... Arnold says ... local history society ... Clearwell Castle and the caves ... extraordinary little coal mines ... amazing church, you *must* make time for that

... Cathedral of the Forest ... Newland ... splendid little pub, marvellous food...'

Freed at last from my sticky cake, I interrupted her. 'It all sounds splendid and I'll enjoy seeing it, but I must ...' I gathered up my bag and tried hard to catch someone's eye to get my bill.

'Oh, you *must* stay and meet Arnold. He's only gone to the DIY place, he'll be along here soon.'

Knowing from bitter experience that bores usually married bores (who else?) I was determined not to get trapped by Arnold, who would doubtless have fascinating things to tell me about the road-fund licence or airport security, or whatever his branch of the Ministry of Transport did. Fortunately the middle-aged lady in the hat suddenly materialised and said, 'Were you the date and walnut?' and gave me a bill.

'I *do* wish I could stay,' I said, with the warmth that only a downright lie can give, 'but I've got an appointment and I mustn't be late. It's been lovely seeing you.'

I backed away, paid the bill and made my escape.

As I sat in the car fastening my seat belt I was aware that I was feeling rather resentful that Ruth hadn't made a single enquiry about *my* life. She didn't even ask what my married name was! Not that I wanted to tell her my life story—heaven forbid!—but still, I felt a little bit niggled.

I drove out of Chepstow and into the Forest. And it *was* a forest and not a wood, dark and somehow forbidding. There were a lot of conifers and Forestry Commission plantations, but also long stretches of broad-leaf trees, just beginning to turn to gold. Very beautiful, really, but not the friendly sort of beauty that our West Somerset woods have. The trees were larger and taller and seemed to encroach on the road, as if, for two pins, they would sweep it away altogether. Tessa started to whine a little in the back and I thought I'd better let them out for a run. I parked on a grass verge by a little lane. There was, on the corner, a low metal road-sign with the name in black on a white ground—strangely urban in such a setting. The sign read 'Miss Grace's Lane'.

I clipped the dog leads on and they pulled me down the lane, snuffling and exploring in the hedges full of dead leaves and interesting smells. The lane was quite short and uninteresting and ended suddenly in a gate with a field beyond. I wondered who on earth Miss Grace had been and why she had given her name to this rather boring little cul-de-sac. Perhaps, surrounded as it was by the intimidating forest, it was the only place she felt comfortable enough to walk in.

I gave the dogs some biscuits and water, put them back in the car and continued my journey. A little further on I saw a small garage and decided that, since I didn't know how far I'd have to go, I'd better fill up with petrol. The brand of petrol was one I'd never heard of but I decided they were all much of a muchness and drew up beside one of the two pumps. Sometimes I have problems with my petrol-locking cap—it suddenly seizes up for no reason at all—and I was wrestling with it when a child came out of the garage. He was a boy of about ten or eleven, small and thin with a pale face and short brown hair that stood up in a spike on the crown. He regarded me with mild contempt, unlocked the petrol cap, unhooked the nozzle of the pump and looked at me enquiringly.

'Oh,' I said, feeling flustered, 'fill it up, please, if you will.'

The child filled the tank, replaced the cap, took a chamois leather from the pocket of his jeans and cleaned the windscreen. Then he went back into the garage and I followed him meekly.

Inside there was a girl—a little older, about twelve—stacking bottles of car shampoo on the shelves. The boy stood beside the electronic till and I said, 'You take credit cards?'

He held out his hand. 'That's right,' he said in what I took to be the local accent. He processed my card with brisk efficiency and gave it back to me.

Another boy, this time very young, certainly

not more than six, came in from the back with a pile of roadmaps which he began to lay out on the counter beside the till. I wanted to say something—I longed to know what had happened to all the grown-ups, what the children were doing there—but they were behaving as if this was their normal way of life, absorbed in everyday tasks, business-like, working in a silence that it seemed somehow impertinent to break.

I put my credit card back in my bag, gave the boy at the till a nervous smile and said, 'Well, thank you, goodbye.'

'Have a nice day,' he said, the cliché sounding strange and outlandish in that accent and in those circumstances.

Decidedly shaken by this encounter I drove on and, not surprisingly, found I had missed the way. The forest still stretched away on either side of the road, but now it was thinner and in among the trees there were sheep—scraggy creatures with bedraggled coats, rummaging among the leaves and bracken. There was no mention of Coleford on the next signpost I got to. I drew up beside it and a heavily laden lorry with the words Tintern Quarry on its side rushed past me. One of the names on the signpost was Clearwell and I remembered that Ruth had mentioned it, I hoped in connection with the marvellous pub, because I suddenly realised that what I *really* wanted was a comforting gin and tonic.

Clearwell was quite a large village; a lot of the houses had been gentrified and there were several little enclaves of new village houses, stone-built with those pointed wooden window-frames they all seem to go in for nowadays. I identified the castle (a nineteenth-century crenellated building, now a hotel) and wondered which of the three pubs to choose. I avoided the largest, hung with a plethora of hanging baskets, the geraniums still in full and exuberant bloom, and made my way into a small one called the Orepool. It was dark inside, but cosy and quite full. I got my drink, ordered some lasagna and went to sit in the corner by the window. I wished I had a book; the other customers stared at me, not in an unfriendly way, but curiously, as if I were of another species or from another planet, then went back to their darts and bar billiards. When the food came I bent my head over my plate, ate it quickly and went over to the bar to pay the bill.

I asked the barman for directions to Coleford.

'You need to go through the village and turn right past the chapel, then up across the Meend,' he said.

'The Meend?'

'The Meend,' he repeated impatiently, 'and you'll find yourself on the Coleford road. You can't miss it.'

As I drove through the village I saw the

church, which was unremarkable—obviously not the one urged upon me by Ruth—and looked about me for a chapel. On the right-hand side I saw a small, vaguely ecclesiastical building with a graveyard behind it, and stopped in amazement. I parked the car and went over to get a better look. It was a very mild autumn and, as I've said, there were still a lot of flowers in bloom, but there in the graveyard was such a blaze of colour that it took my breath away. I opened the tall iron gate and went inside.

It was a large churchyard with a small chapel at one end, obviously used solely for funerals since the graveyard was some way from the church. Around the edge, in front of the boundary wall, someone had made a vast, circular raised bed and this was filled with late flowering dahlias, chrysanthemums, rudbeckia and Michaelmas daisies. That was not all. All along the perfectly kept path were small beds also filled with flowers and every grave that had no vase of flowers of its own or layer of chippings had been planted with marigolds and brilliant yellow daisies. The effect was stunning. I walked a little way along the path and came upon an old duffle coat which had been thrown down on the ground, and, lying beside it, a small black dog who was guarding it. She had, laid out neatly on the ground, a bowl of water, a bone and a handful of dog biscuits. The dog, who had been chewing the bone, looked up as I approached, then she got up and came towards me, wagging her tail. I put out a hand to stroke her glossy coat and she rolled over so that I could pat her fat stomach. I spoke to her and petted her and then suddenly she scrambled to her feet and rushed down the path towards a figure coming towards me.

Just for a moment I felt frightened. The man approaching was very strange. He was tall and very thin, with tangled grey hair down below his shoulders and a grey beard to his waist—it was as disconcerting as suddenly coming upon an Old Testament prophet. He was wearing a collarless shirt with the sleeves rolled up, a navy waistcoat that had once belonged to a suit and old khaki trousers tied at the knee with binder cord. I hesitated. It was very quiet with no one in sight and the man looked so odd that my instincts told me I should hurry away, back to the car and safety, but then I saw the dog leaping up at him and the gentle way he patted her head and, perhaps irrationally, I stopped being frightened.

I walked towards him, calling out, 'Good afternoon.'

'Afternoon, missus.' His voice was non-committal.

'Is that your dog? She's in beautiful condition.'

'She's a good dog is Trixie.'

He seemed pleased and I continued, 'And is this beautiful place all your work?'

'It is. It's what I do, look after the graveyard.'

'I've never seen one like it.'

'No, folks do say that.'

'And do you do it all on your own? It's quite magnificent.'

'I like to see the graveyard look well.' He paused and then volunteered, 'They didn't buy none of those plants, it's all what people have give me when I do their gardens.'

'That's wonderful. And all the old graves planted like this.'

'I don't like the old ones to think they've been forgotten,' he said.

Trixie had been rolling at his feet, but then she broke away and came back to me delighted to have a second person's attention. As I bent down to stroke her, my eye was caught by a new grave, the earth on it still roughly turned and with one wreath (white chrysanthemums, now turning brown at the edges) laid at its head. Stuck into the earth at the end of the grave nearest to the path was a wooden peg, on which was written in biro the inscription 'Edith Mary Rossiter'.

CHAPTER TWELVE

As I straightened up something of what I felt must have shown in my face because the man said, 'Are you all right, missus?'

I tried to think coherently.

'Yes ... That is, I've had a bit of a shock. That'—I pointed to the place—'is the grave of someone I knew—I hadn't expected to find her here.'

'You'd better sit down. Here'—he took my arm gently—'sit down on the seat until you feel proper.'

I found that I was shaking—shock, I suppose—and clenched my hands tightly to pull myself together. The man looked at me with some concern and the dog sat close by my feet as if in sympathy. After a while I felt more myself and said, 'The lady who is buried over there—do you know anything about her?'

He pulled at his beard, considering the question before he replied and then said, 'The funeral were about a couple of weeks ago. She were the lady staying with that foreign gentleman and his sister in the holiday cottage up on the Meend.'

'Foreign?' I asked. 'What sort of foreign?'

'That I couldn't say. Foreign. Talks funny. Proper English, but funny, you know what I mean. Not that I saw him more than a couple of times and never saw the sister at all—an invalid, that Molly Phillips in the Post Office says, though I don't know how she knows, because I don't reckon she's ever set eyes on her, nor on this lady either.' He gestured towards the grave. 'Nobody did. The ladies

191

didn't go out at all and the gentleman, he only went into Coleford in the car to get the shopping.'

'Didn't anyone see them?'

'No. Nobody goes up there much, it don't lead nowhere. Reg Lydden might have seen them when he went up on to the Meend to see to his sheep. But he didn't say nothing about it. He don't say much about nothing, do Reg Lydden.'

'Is the foreign gentleman still here?' I asked.

'That's right, still here, him and his sister. Won't be for long, though. Said he's going away next week. Give me money to keep up the grave, though I didn't want none. I like to see the old graveyard look nice. He asked the vicar to see to the stone. Can't put up no stone until the ground's settled. That's why it's marked, you see.' He indicated the wooden peg.

'Yes, I see. Tell me, do you know his name?'

'His name?' The man looked surprised at my question. 'I don't rightly recall it—it were a foreign name. Van something.'

'Van!'

'That's right. Foreign,' he explained patiently, 'like I said. I've got it writ down, he put it on a bit of paper for me. I've got it somewhere in the house.'

'Can you tell me how to get to the cottage where he lives?' I asked.

'You want to go up there?'

'Yes, I—I'd like to ask about my friend.'

'Yes, well, it's not far. You go along this road for about half a mile and then you'll see a narrow lane going off to the right. Real steep, it is. Follow that on for another half mile and you'll see Brooks Cottage on the left, right on the top of the hill. You can't miss it, nothing else up there. Miserable place in winter. Old Jackie Brooks used to be snowed up half the year when he lived there.'

'Thank you so much,' I said. 'You've been very kind.'

I felt in my handbag and found a five-pound note.

'Please take this,' I said, thrusting it into his hand. 'No,' I continued when he protested, 'I'm so glad you're looking after her grave. If you like, get something for your little dog, some extra biscuits or something. She'd have liked that. She loved animals.'

I stood for a moment looking down at the grave and then walked quickly back to the car.

I found the lane and drove up the steep slope and out on to what I decided must be the Meend. It was rough common land, mostly covered with bracken and with a few scattered windblown hawthorns and elder bushes. Several defeated-looking sheep strayed across the road, unconcerned or unused to traffic, and a few were drinking at one of the pools of dark, brackish water beside it. In front of me on the top of the hill I saw a cottage, standing on its own, silhouetted against the sky.

I stopped the car. Everywhere was very quiet and still. There was no birdsong, no wind, no sound of any human activity. The Meend stretched away for some distance on either side and far away to the left I could see the vague greyish shape of the Welsh Black Mountains which seemed to melt into a greyer sky. Now, having got so far, I wasn't sure if I wanted to go on. *Van*—it seemed incredible. I had been so sure that Marion had nothing to do with Mrs Rossiter's disappearance. My mind was confused and I didn't seem able to think properly. I sat for a few moments, unable to make any movement, forward or back. Then Tris, excited by a sheep moving beside the car, uttered a sharp bark and I started the car again and went on up the hill.

I stood for a moment at the gate, looking up at the cottage. It was built of grey stone, probably a miner's cottage and quite small, but an extension had been built on to the side and there had been some attempt to make a garden at the front with shrubs and paved flagstones. As I looked, I thought I saw the curtains in the downstairs window moving, as if someone was looking out from behind them. I thought of Michael's warning about plunging into things and of what I might find, and I hesitated. Then I took a deep breath and knocked on the door. My mind was a complete blank. I had no idea what I was going to say to Van and whoever else was there; I would just let things happen.

I waited for what seemed like ages and then I knocked again. It was, I noticed, a black iron knocker, old and worn underneath—the original, I supposed, and not a modern reproduction. The door was suddenly opened, not by Van, not, indeed, by anyone I had ever seen before, but by an elderly man.

He was tall and very thin, his face deeply suntanned and with eyes that were still a clear, bright blue. He stood looking at me without speaking, his gaze steady and enquiring. I found myself talking quickly and not very coherently.

'Oh, I'm sorry to bother you. I'm looking for someone who can give me news of Mrs Rossiter, Mrs Edith Rossiter. I believe she's been staying here. I'm an old friend—Sheila Malory—we've been so worried...'

He opened the door wider.

'You'd better come in,' he said.

His accent was strange; I couldn't place it. I followed him into the cottage and he shut the door behind me.

'Please sit down, Mrs Malory.'

Trying to look relaxed and unconcerned, I sat down in one of the small chintz-covered armchairs on either side of the fireplace. The room was pleasantly furnished in a cottagey sort of way and there were several beautifully arranged bowls of flowers set on small tables or on the broad window-sills. These I found somehow reassuring. People, I told myself, who had committed unspeakable crimes would not, surely, spend time arranging flowers.

'Can I get you some tea, or coffee, perhaps?' the man asked politely.

'No. No, thank you. I've just had lunch, really.'

There was a silence while I tried to think how to put the questions I had to ask. Suddenly the man smiled. His rather austere face was transformed; it was a warm, open, *friendly* smile and I found myself instinctively smiling back.

'So you're Sheila,' he said. 'I'm really glad to meet you at last. My name's Christian Vanderlinden.'

'Christian ...' All sorts of bells were ringing in my head.

'Edie always calls—called—me Chris.'

'You're South African?' I asked.

'Born and brought up there. I worked there until just after the war, then I went to Canada. I've lived there ever since.'

That explained his strange accent. My eye was suddenly caught by an object on one of the small tables, something I recognised.

'The gazelle!' I exclaimed. I went and picked it up, holding it in my hand as I had done many times since I was a child, feeling the smoothness, the warmth, almost, of the ivory. 'So she *did* take it with her!'

'I gave it to Edie on her eighteenth birthday.'

'Then you—' I broke off and sat down.

'Please, will you explain what has happened? I'm so confused.'

'Yes,' he said, 'I'll explain, but first I will pour us both a glass of wine. Yes, I know it's the wrong time of day,' he smiled again, 'but we will both feel more at ease with glasses in our hands.'

He went into the kitchen and I got up and looked out of the window. From the cottage, high on the top of the hill, the view was magnificent, hills and valleys rolling away into the distance. The sun had come out from behind the clouds now, bathing the landscape in soft autumnal light, so that it looked like a painting by Richard Wilson. Christian Vanderlinden came back with two glasses and a bottle on a tray and poured us each a glass of white wine. He was right; we both relaxed, almost like old acquaintances.

'Edie's father,' Christian said, 'was a rich man. He didn't think I was a good enough catch'—here his voice grated harshly—'for his daughter. He was right, I suppose, in worldly terms. I was a young engineer, just starting to make my way. But I loved Edie and she loved me. For another father that might have been enough, but not for him.'

'What about her mother?' I asked.

'She wouldn't have stopped us getting married, but she had nothing to do with it. The poor wretched little creature couldn't call her soul her own, didn't like South Africa, just wanted to go back to England to live like they used to in the old days before he made his money. She was frightened of him—they were all frightened of him, her and both the girls. He used to fly into these terrible rages, there was no reasoning with him.'

I thought of Alan.

'He flew into a rage with me when I went to tell him that Edie and I wanted to get married. Shouted the place down, said we must never see each other again, turned me out of the house—called the servants to say that they must never let me in if I called. It was brutal and humiliating.'

His eyes were cold and I saw that he was unconsciously clenching his hands as he remembered. After a moment he continued.

'We managed to meet secretly a few times. Poor little Edie, she was so terrified that he'd find out. I begged her to come away with me, but she wouldn't. It wasn't because of the money.' He gazed at me earnestly. 'She never cared anything for that; she would have happily starved with me. She was afraid that he'd come after us—she wasn't twenty-one—and she couldn't bear the scenes and his violent temper. Not just for her, but the old man would have taken it out on her mother and her sister, too. She said their lives wouldn't be worth living.'

He got up and went over to the window, leaning on the sill. His back was to me and his voice was muffled.

'I was young, too, and I was very bitter. I said that if she wouldn't come with me then she didn't love me, that she only cared for wealth and position. I said a lot of stupid things. And she cried. I remember how she cried.'

He turned round and faced me.

'So,' he said, 'I went away. Off to Rhodesia, to the Copper Belt. I did well, made quite a bit of money, quite a name for myself as an engineer. When I got back to Durban they'd gone. He'd taken them back to England. I asked around and found their address and wrote to her. The letter came back, marked "Return to Sender".'

'How cruel!' I exclaimed.

'He was an expert. Not violence—he never hit them—but worse, he ruined their lives and destroyed their spirit. I didn't give up, though. The next year I had to go to England on business, so I went to find her. They were living in this great old house in the country, and I put up at the hotel in the nearest village— Dulverton, it was called, I remember—and made some enquiries. It wasn't difficult to find out; people down there seemed to like a bit of gossip and it was all still fairly fresh in their minds. Edie had been married just a few months before. From what I gathered she hadn't wanted to marry the man. He had a bad reputation, another evil-tempered man— everything she dreaded. He was one of those newly poor landed gentry, so they said, who only married her for her father's money.'

'He was a horrible man,' I said. 'I hated him.'

'You can imagine how I felt. I had to see her. I went off for a walk through the woods, trying to work out what to do for the best, how to rescue her. I walked a long way. It was about this time of the year, but cold and misty. I heard a dog barking; it sounded in trouble so I went towards where the sound was coming from.

'He was lying on the ground, his gun half underneath him and his poor dog—a spaniel—standing beside him, barking its head off. It was him, Edie's father. I just stood there looking down at him. There was a lot of blood and not much left of his face, but I knew it was him; it was a face that had been in my mind's eye for too long for me to be mistaken. He was dead. I'm sure he was dead.'

He looked away from me again and repeated, 'I'm sure he was dead.'

Abruptly he left the window and sat down in his chair.

'I thought I heard noises and I ran away. I thought well—that if anyone found me standing by his body, they would think I'd killed him. God knows I had good cause. But, you see, the awful thing was, I ran *right* away, I didn't try to find Edie. I didn't beg her to leave that man and come away with me. I just ran, right the way back to Durban. I let her down.'

'No,' I said. 'She wouldn't have gone with you, however much she wanted to. She wouldn't have broken her marriage vows. That wasn't her way. It would just have been more anguish for her.'

'I guess you're right. She's—she was that sort of person. So,' he continued, 'I stayed in South Africa and then after the war I moved to Canada. My sister Olive had lost her husband in the war so she came to keep house for me.'

'You never married?' I asked.

'No. It was only Edie for me. If I couldn't have her, then I didn't want anyone else. Does that sound silly?'

'No,' I said warmly. 'It sounds splendid.'

He smiled. 'Olive and I travelled quite a bit—never to England, I couldn't face that. And last year—now here's a very strange thing—last year, when we were in Paris in some café, I picked up a copy of *The Times* and there, what should catch my eye but an announcement of *his* death. "Colonel Julian Rossiter, The Manor House, Stone Down, Somerset".'

I remembered Thelma had taken over all the arrangements. It was she who had decided on cremation and on the precise charity to which donations should be sent.

Christian Vanderlinden continued, 'I wrote to Edie, quite a formal letter, just saying that I'd seen the announcement and asking how she was. They forwarded the letter to that Home.'

201

There was a world of scorn in the last word. 'Fancy putting Edie in a Home, as if she was an old woman!'

'I know,' I said, 'it shouldn't have happened.'

'That bitch of a daughter!'

His vehemence shocked me and then I thought for a moment and said, 'Yes, you're right. Thelma *is* a bitch, she always has been. I'm so used to thinking about her as a comic sort of character—Horrible Thelma, which is what my friend Rosemary and I always used to call her when we were young. But one should really look at her dispassionately and see just what a vilely manipulative person she is. She fools so many people with that saccharine manner ... And Alan's not much better.'

He gave me a grateful look and said, 'Edie said that she didn't know how she would have got through, if it hadn't been for you and your mother.'

'She asked for so little,' I said, 'just someone to love and be loved by.'

'Is that so little?' he asked. 'Perhaps, sometimes, it is a lot to ask. Certainly it is the greatest gift that anyone can give—I know that.'

'Did she reply to your letter?'

'Oh, yes. We wrote to each other several times. Then I went down to see her. I left Olive in London and went on my own. It was wonderful. After all she'd been through she was still my Edie, just as sweet and loving as she'd been all those years ago. I wanted her to leave that place there and then, but she wouldn't. She was afraid that daughter of hers would come after us ... So I made a little plan. She would pretend to go shopping, let them think that she'd be back, and then meet me and Olive and we'd come down here, where no one would find her. So that's what we did. She felt badly, though, about *you*, knowing that you'd worry, but she didn't tell you because she knew her daughter would be on to you straight away and she didn't want you to have to lie for her.'

'No,' I said. 'If I'd known, I *might* have broken under Thelma's cross-examination! But,' I asked, 'why here? I mean, I know it's remote, but why this particular spot?'

'You'll laugh. It was a silly, sentimental sort of thing. When we were young, back in Durban, we used to read poetry together—Wordsworth in particular—and one of our favourites was his poem written near Tintern Abbey. We always said that one day we'd go to England and read the poem there, where he wrote it.'

'And did you?'

'Yes, just before ...'

'I'm so glad. "Little, nameless, unremembered acts of kindness and of love"—yes, that was dear Mrs Rossiter. So what happened? Was it a heart attack?'

'Yes. Quite sudden—thank God. The doctor

came at once but it was all over.'

'I'm sorry...'

'These last few months have been wonderful. She's ... she felt it too, she said so over and over. It could never make up for all the years we lost, but we found something at the end...'

'And now you're going back to Canada, you and your sister?'

'Yes, next week. I'm sorry Olive can't meet you—she would have liked to very much, after hearing all the things that Edie told her. They got on so well, almost like sisters. But she's not very well at the moment, some sort of virus, the doctor says, and she's stuck in bed. Not a good patient!'

'I'm so sorry—and I'm very sorry to miss seeing her.'

We chatted for a little while longer and then, as I gathered up my bag and prepared to go, he asked, 'How did you find me?'

I explained about Michael seeing the name of the solicitor in the *London Gazette* and how I'd come upon the old man in the graveyard.

'I'm sorry,' he said, 'that you had that dreadful shock. It must have been really bad. But I'm so glad that you came here and that we've had this talk. I was going to write to you when I got back to Ontario, but this is so much better.'

He came with me to the door and, as we stood looking out over the valley, he quoted, smiling,

' "These hedgerows, hardly hedgerows, little lines
Of sportive wood run wild."

'I'll never forget this place.'

I held out my hand. 'Goodbye, and thank you for giving her those last months.'

He took my hand in both of his and clasped it warmly. As I went down the path I could feel his eyes upon me, but when I got to the car and turned to wave goodbye he had closed the door and was gone.

I drove across the Meend and took a winding road that led me down to the river. I went on, through Llandogo until, across the Wye, I could see the outline of the abbey ruins silhouetted against a pink and gold sky. It was breathtakingly beautiful and I hoped that Mrs Rossiter and Christian Vanderlinden had seen it at such a moment. I pulled into a lay-by and sat for a while looking across at Wordsworth's steep woods and lofty cliffs and hearing his words echoing in my head:

For I have learned
To look on nature, not as in the hour
Of thoughtless youth; but hearing oftentimes
The still, sad music of humanity,
Nor harsh nor grating, though of ample power

To chasten and subdue.

And there I said a last goodbye to my old friend. Then, as I started on the long drive home, I put the car radio on and tried to lose myself in the ordinary, commonplace things that make up our real life.

CHAPTER THIRTEEN

Next morning I went to see Mrs Jankiewicz. As I told her about my journey and what I had discovered she sat silently, her hands in her lap. She was so unresponsive that I suddenly looked at her and exclaimed, 'You knew! You knew where she'd gone all the time! That's why you would never talk about it!'

She leaned forward and took my hand in a rare gesture of affection.

'I'm sorry, Sheila, but I could tell no one. I promise not to tell anyone, even you. She would not have told me, but I go into her room that day he was there and she have to explain who he is, and, well, I am not a stupid. I can see how happy she is, she has to go with him. Was a miracle.'

'Yes,' I said. 'But oh, how I *wish* she'd had just a little longer.'

'The length of time, it does not matter. Enough that it came.'

'You're right, I suppose. It's just that I'm greedy for her...'

'Her time had come. Time to make that final journey—is the shortest one we make, from this world to the next. Soon, I too will make it.'

'No,' I protested, 'not you. You're so strong, you won't leave us all yet!'

But, as I looked at her, I saw that she too was frail and old.

*   *   *

Life went on. I began research on another book and, with the horrid imminence of the festive season, found myself submerged in arrangements about Christmas Fayres, baking endless trays of mince pies for the freezer against the day when they would be demanded of me by the organisers of events for various good causes. I had just returned from a morning of pricing Fancy Goods for one of the stalls—always a delicate matter when the maker of the object to be priced is standing at one's elbow, ready to take offence if she (it is usually a she) considers it has been undervalued. Rosemary and I had also been putting up the trestle tables, borrowed from the boy scouts and always a source of friction.

'Honestly,' Rosemary said, 'you'd think they were inlaid with gold *leaf* the way George Hood goes on about them. Anyone would think we were going to *dance* on them, not just cover them with woolly bedsocks and matinée coats. "You will take *care* of them, won't you?"' She mimicked the Scoutmaster's voice. 'He really is a terrible old woman.'

'Well, he does have a mother,' I said.

Rosemary sighed. 'Haven't we all!'

'Oh dear,' I said. 'What's she up to now?'

'It's Christmas. Jilly wants Jack and me to go to them for the baby's first Christmas—you know how silly one is—a tree and all those little presents—although Delia is *far* too young to know what's going on. Do you know, Roger's making her a doll's-house?'

'Bless him,' I said. 'Peter bought Michael a train set for *his* first Christmas. So what's the problem?'

'Well, Jilly and Roger have very sweetly invited Mother too—though goodness knows she'd only cast a blight on the proceedings— and she won't go. What she wants is for me to do the whole thing for everyone, as I do it every year, so that she can criticise everything. She couldn't do that if we went to Jilly's because she's just a *little* in awe of Roger. It's something to do with him being the son of a bishop.'

'Oh, but you *must* go to Jilly's,' I said. 'Apart from everything else, you really do deserve to have your Christmas dinner cooked by someone else for a change!'

'Jack agrees with you, says we must go. But what can I do about Mother? I can't leave her to have Christmas on her own.'

'Serve her right. Anyway, she's got Elsie to look after her.'

'Oh I know, but still ... She keeps saying that this might be her last Christmas.'

'Oh, for goodness' sake, she's as strong as a horse!'

'Yes, well ... but she is old and you never know. I'd feel so awful. Anyway, what would people think!'

I imagined Mrs Dudley's plaintive voice: 'No, never mind me, I shall do very well on my own—I do feel that young people like to lead their own lives ... Ah well, they'll be old themselves one day...'

'You mustn't let her blackmail you like this,' I said. But I knew that it was a lost cause and that Rosemary and Jack would be having Mrs Dudley for Christmas as they had always done. Blessed are the meek, I suppose, but it seems to me that they have an awfully long time to wait for their inheritance.

'Perhaps we might go to see Jilly and Roger at New Year,' Rosemary said tentatively.

It was quite a tiring morning and I was glad to get home. I fed the animals and made myself a mushroom omelette. I had just slid it, all warm and buttery, on to the plate when the phone rang. For a moment I thought of ignoring it, but then, as I always do, I thought it might be Michael with some problem, so I resignedly put the omelette into the Aga warming oven and picked up the receiver.

'Sheila?' It was Thelma. 'I've just got back from New York—last week, actually—to find this *appalling* news about Mother.'

So she knew that her mother was dead. I supposed the solicitor had written.

'This wicked business about the will!'

'The will?'

It occurred to me that I had forgotten all about the new will and the solicitor in Coleford. Somehow, what I had found out that day in the cottage on the Meend made it seem irrelevant.

'Yes, this new will of my mother's. She's dead. Heart attack—there was a doctor's certificate. I always told you that she wasn't well enough to live on her own. *Now*, perhaps, you will all see that I was right. But just before she died she made this new will. Quite preposterous. Of course she couldn't break the Trust, thank God. I shall get Grandfather's money, but all the rest—her own money...'

Here she broke off, possibly to draw breath, possibly from emotion.

'Yes?' I prompted her.

'Well, there are a few bequests. You get that Regency desk, by the way. It's quite a nice piece—I had it valued—but it's been restored and wouldn't fetch more than about seven hundred and fifty pounds at auction. That mad Polish woman gets the rest of the things in her room at West Lodge. Alan'—here her voice became shriller—'*he* gets a very large sum for

210

that ridiculous expedition with that scheming American woman. By the way, did I tell you that he's turned up again? He was in America with *her* all the time! The rest of her fortune—and it's well over a million—goes to this man, Christian Vanderlinden.'

'What!'

'Yes. *I'd* never heard of him either. No address, just the Bank of Canada in London. It seems he was someone she knew in Durban when she was a girl. He went to see her at West Lodge—what Mrs Wilmot was thinking of to let in a person like that!—and persuaded her to go off with him and his sister. Did you ever *hear* of such a thing! Well, there could only be one reason for that! Especially since he wouldn't let her tell anyone where she was. She always was a fool, she'd do whatever anyone asked without question.'

'Yes,' I said, 'she was very biddable.'

'Exactly, *biddable*.' Thelma repeated the word with relish. 'A biddable fool. Well. I wanted to fight the will—undue influence and so forth—but Simon says that the costs would be horrendous, even if he was acting for me. It would drag on and on and there'd be precious little left.'

'Jarndyce and Jarndyce,' I murmured.

'What?'

'Nothing. So what will you do?'

'Simon and I are going to South Africa next week to sort out the details of the Trust relating

211

to the property there. I think we must get the money out of there if we can. Simon says the situation isn't as stable as he'd like.'

'I see.'

'Well, I thought I must just let you know what's happened and what a dreadful mess she's made of things. Oh, by the way, she's buried in some peculiar place in Gloucestershire. I forget the name, I'll get my secretary to let you have it. I know you have a *thing* about graves and so forth. I'll be in touch.'

In a sort of daze I returned to the kitchen, took my omelette out of the oven and put it on the table. I looked at the brown, shrivelled thing before me, pushed it aside and made myself a cup of tea. I didn't really feel like eating.

All that sentimental nonsense, the faithful-unto-death bit, the Wordsworth ... Even if he hadn't actually killed her (and it seemed that the heart attack was genuine enough) he had still deceived her, luring her away, letting her tell no one where she was going—and all for the money. As I sometimes feel when I've eaten too much chocolate, so, after my wallow in sentimentality, I felt rather sick. I also felt an absolute and utter fool.

*　　　*　　　*

Christmas came and went and after a while I

212

put the whole affair out of my mind. Michael went back to London, leaving behind his motorbike, but with a small secondhand car, presenting me with a whole new category of things to worry about. One particularly gloomy morning—the sky was steel grey, the ground was frozen hard and there was a vicious east wind—I went into the hall to get the post. There were the usual post-Christmas bills and a letter with a Canadian stamp, which I presumed was one of Sophie's chatty and entertaining accounts of her busy life. I poured myself a second cup of coffee and saw that the address was typed and there was no return address on the envelope. When I drew the closely written sheets from the envelope I could scarcely believe my eyes.

16 Valley View, Nepean, Ontario

My dearest Sheila,
I can imagine what a shock this letter will be to you and I'm so sorry about that, but I did so much want you to know that I am well and oh so happy.

Perhaps I had better tell you about things as they happened. As Chris will have told you, he wrote to me to say that he had seen the announcement of Julian's death. I can't tell you what an excitement it was hearing from him after all those years and when he said he wanted to come and see me I almost

213

said no. I know it was foolish, but I half wanted him to remember me as a young girl and not an old woman. Fortunately I did say yes and he came. Oh Sheila, it was wonderful—it was just as if we had never been parted. I knew we had to be together but I was so frightened of what Thelma might do to stop us. I do wish that I could have told you—I had to tell Mrs Jankiewicz, but I knew she would never say anything. Chris told you how we managed things and how marvellous those months were in that heavenly place. It was wonderful to meet Olive at last—Father had never allowed me to see any of Chris's family or friends—we got on so well.

Chris and I were married by special licence at the Registrar's Office in Gloucester and I was to go back to Ontario with them. As his wife I could travel on Chris's passport, you see. I'm so glad that Olive was at the wedding. I didn't have anything new to wear—well, I was frightened to go into any of the shops just in case I met someone I knew—I'd been wearing some of Olive's clothes because I couldn't bring anything with me! But it was a lovely wedding and we went back to the cottage and Chris opened a bottle of champagne that he'd bought and we had some nice smoked salmon sandwiches he'd got at Marks and Spencer! Olive said that when we got back to Ontario we'd have a real celebration. Poor Olive. We had to wait for the papers to come through—the passport and tickets and so forth—but before they arrived the poor soul died. She wasn't very strong and she was some years older than Chris. It was a heart attack and very quick. We stood there looking down at her and Chris said a little prayer.

Then I had an idea. It was rather shocking and I was a bit ashamed of it, but Olive was dead and I didn't think she'd mind. I said to Chris that since we had hardly spoken to anyone while we'd been at the cottage nobody knew which of us was which. So why didn't we pretend that Olive was me and that *I* was dead? If we buried her as Edith Rossiter then Thelma would never be able to get at me again!

Chris was a bit doubtful—he's such an honest man, with such high principles—but I persuaded him and it all worked beautifully. I honestly don't think that Olive would mind lying at rest in that beautiful churchyard, and she was such a kind soul I think she would have been glad to give me that peace of mind. Chris felt very bad, Sheila, at deceiving you. When you knocked at the door and I looked through the curtains and saw you standing there I almost rushed out there and then to give you a hug like we used to. But we'd come so far and I thought we must go through with it, though it broke my heart to see you looking so sad as I stood at the bedroom window and saw you going down the garden path.

I expect that by now you will have heard from Thelma about my will. It must have been a very nasty surprise for her! Chris was very worried and upset when I told him how I was going to leave the money—he has a strong sense of family and, even though Thelma and Alan haven't been very loving children, I think he was rather shocked at what I had done. But honestly, Sheila, after all the misery that money has caused, I thought it was time it did a bit of good for a change. Chris and Olive have always done so much for the community here—raising funds for this and that—it will be really marvellous to be able to help. We won't spend a penny of it on ourselves. Chris is quite well off—he did very well in his job and I'm so proud of what he achieved—and has plenty of money for us to live on. Father's money has only brought me unhappiness— and poor Mother, too—so it will be wonderful to think it can make other people happier. I left Alan the amount he wanted for that expedition—I know his motives were selfish, but it might do a little good for others—and Thelma will have all her grandfather's money from the Trust (she's very like him in many ways so it seems right, somehow), so, really, she has no reason to complain—though I'm sure she will!

I made the will before Olive died, of course, and I thought then that after a while I would be presumed dead (is that the phrase?) and the will would be proved in the usual way. But having a death certificate in my name has made it all much easier. So wasn't I clever! Dear Chris was very doubtful about it all at first but I think he's coming round to it now, especially as we have a joint account and I write all the cheques so that no one can say that he's a fortune hunter! You see how independent I'm getting these days! But, really, I seem to have taken on a new lease of life. Chris says that if he knew how bossy I'd become he'd never have married me!

The people in Nepean (I called it Nepeen at first, but it's Nepean—three syllables!) are so nice and friendly and Chris's house is lovely. They're so hospitable. Soon after we arrived a group of his friends gave a lovely party for us at Emilio's, which is a very nice restaurant not far from here. Chris does a lot of work for the local hospital and for a sort of help-line (rather like our Samaritans) and I am helping Emma (who is our next-door neighbour) with her basket supper to help raise funds for St Mark's—that's the Anglican Church we go to. Oh, Sheila, I'm having such fun. I never knew life could be so wonderful. I'm so very lucky.

I must finish now and let Chris take this to the post. It's very snowy here, but the house is lovely and warm, and everything looks very pretty. Yesterday I saw the young people were skating at the outdoor rink at the Civic Centre. People do seem to enjoy themselves more over here. Perhaps one day you could come over and see us. Wouldn't that be lovely? Tell Mrs Jankiewicz all about this, please. I don't think I'd better risk a letter to West Lodge!! Write to me soon and let me know that you forgive me and tell me all the Taviscombe gossip.

My dearest love to you.

Your old friend, E.V.

Scrawled at the bottom in a different hand was a brief note: 'Please do forgive me—I hated to deceive you that day. We very much want you to come and see us, just so that you can see how happy we are! C.V.'

I put the letter down on the table and sat staring at it for some time—so long, in fact, that Tessa, worried by my unaccustomed stillness, nudged my leg with her nose and whined softly.

*　　　*　　　*

I took the letter down to West Lodge and read

218

it to Mrs Jankiewicz. When I had finished I saw that she had tears in her eyes.

'Is good,' she said, smiling. 'Is very good. When I see them together I know it will be right for her. I am never wrong!'

She rummaged in the large black leather handbag that she always kept beside her and found a handkerchief and blew her nose vigorously. Then she drew a letter from the recesses of the bag and said, 'And now I have the news for you. My Adam is coming to see me soon. He writes that he is thinking of giving up Cambridge.'

'Oh, surely not!' I exclaimed. 'What will he do?'

'He has seen many programmes about Poland on TV and he wishes to go to Warsaw to work there in our country. He wishes to come to see me so we can talk about Poland and he says he asks my advice.'

'And what will you tell him?' I asked.

She shook her head. She was sitting bolt upright; her head was erect and her eyes were sparkling. She was the Mrs Jankiewicz I had always known.

'I do not know. We talk. I tell him about the old days. I tell him about his ancestors in Poland, many generations ago. He will decide himself. But'—her face softened into a smile—'he comes to ask me. I am not old and useless—there are still things I can do.'

'Yes,' I replied, 'both you and Mrs Rossiter. We still need you.'

'Thanks God,' said Mrs Jankiewicz.

We hope you have enjoyed this Large Print book. Other Chivers Press or G.K. Hall Large Print books are available at your library or directly from the publishers. For more information about current and forthcoming titles, please call or write, without obligation, to:

Chivers Press Limited
Windsor Bridge Road
Bath BAS 3AX
England
Tel. (0225) 335336

OR

G.K. Hall
P.O. Box 159
Thorndike, ME 04986
USA
Tel. (800) 223–6121
(207) 948–2962
(in Maine and Canada, call collect)

All our Large Print titles are designed for easy reading, and all our books are made to last.